"Bewitching and powerful; these stories strike hard and leave you reeling."

Cat Hellisen, author of "King of the Hollow Dark"

"A scintillating cache of stories that sparkle with imagination, tenderness and hard-won truths."

Neil Williamson, author of Queen of Clouds

"A very impressive short story collection with a huge range of versatility, scope and yet always finding a way of delivering its themes that make the reader think about what they've just been reading. I loved the emotional range and surprises these tales told and strongly recommend this to be picked up. An author to watch out for."

www.runalongtheshelves.net

UNDER

THE

MOON

Collected Speculative Fiction

E.M. FAULDS

A CIP catalogue record is available from the British Library

www.ghostmothpress.com

ISBN-13: 978-1-7396851-1-9

CONTENTS

BLESSED STREET

She could place her hand there, on the girl's ankle. Just there, and let the goodness flow in, stop the tremors. Instead, Jessi pulled the corner of the blanket down to where the mattress met the iron cot, tucked it in safe. She could help. Get some light inside that one, maybe calm her.

They'd never let her.

The girl in the bed was young, just reaching up towards womanhood, but here she was sweating, trembling, eyes shut, jaw clenched. Row upon row of Red Dog patients, struggling against their bedding, waiting for their body to overcome the spell. Or for their cots to become their biers; that far too possible. The smell of acid, the laundry in the back, something metallic, perhaps the hot water urn boiling dry again. The sound of groans and retching. The clouds of despair. It was a place of perdition, and one Jessi couldn't fight. Could she?

'Get those buckets changed,' the Clinic Mother said, and Jessi jumped, glad she hadn't tried anything now. 'I'm out to ask the Council for alms again.' The older woman crossed between the cots to leave, her starched

E.M. Faulds

skirts rustling, stiffness permeating her whole being. A passerby might hold her to be a cold-blooded woman. Jessi understood it, though. You had to make your face a board, your movements brusque and efficient. You had to keep some flint in your spine, or the shroud of sorrow could wrap you up, not let you go. And asking for alms from the Chistham Council of Worthies required tenacity.

They tried to keep the Blessed Street Clinic good, despite dire lack of money. Just her, the Clinic Mother, and three other folk who'd more heart than sense to come here and fight a losing battle. Jessi'd thrown in a few picols of her pay from mornings cleaning houses to buy oats for the porage, all some of the mage-sick could countenance. Just to watch it come back up in a hot heave of acid.

Not all of them made it, the ones who shook and vomited. Some gave up the ghost. Some staggered out, still in agony, to look for an easier way. Not that there was one. Each time, they left a space for someone new. Some got through it, weak but themselves again, only to end up looking for another mage, winding another dose of the spell round their heads, and back here in a never-ending circle of self-hate. Very few made it out proper, free for good.

The girl in the bed shook, that small but violent movement. It was a violence done to her by those who wove the spell. There weren't many ways of stopping it. Not for the low-streets poor, anyway. They had to ride it out, hope it shivered out of their bodies and left them sane.

Having healing magic and not being able to use it was a hardness Jessi could never reconcile. Watching over someone who'd methodically tried to dismantle themselves with Red Dog was another. Watching it, she felt cruel. But it was all she could do.

She had her ways, though, to keep herself from walking out the door and down the beach to jump right into the waves. Thought about sweet things, like Tam's eyes.

Tam, did he look at her the way she wanted him to? Jessi thought she saw a flash there, a recognition of the spark inside. His want looking back at hers, him wanting to touch her as much as she wanted him to do it. But she might be letting herself fancy the thought. She'd have to look him in the eye again, soon. Find out more. Maybe he looked at all the girls like that. Maybe he didn't mean it as a kindness, just a hunger like these Redheads hungered for the spell to come wrap them up. They didn't love it. They needed it. It was different.

The Red Dog was a widow-geist over all these cots, the way it called to them, pretended to be an answer. 'It makes you feel good,' was all it took for some. For others, the rest of their lives had shambled into a heap of abandoned hopes, unpayable debts, and sundered loves, and it sent them running to the mages for the secret to happiness. Or at least to numbness. 'I just don't want this pain anymore,' was enough for them. So, they took the spell, and it spun them up like a caterpillar in silk for a while. But then it left them, and every time it left them worse.

*

End of her shift, Yvette finally come in, flapping and late, Jessi guilty with relief at being able to go. Out onto Blessed Street. Right turn, up to the bridge at the foot of the Lofts to look down into the river again. She could never explain this need to come here, to look down over the wooden guardrail silvered by years of hands, onto the foam-laced green that poured off the weir. And to let her cares go for the moment, let her mind plunge into the churn, to be swept, drawn along.

Let yourself slack like the tide-water going out. That's what her mother had told her when she'd asked about magic. All you needed, she'd told her, was to let go. And it was harder than it sounded. Maybe this was practice. Maybe the only thing keeping her whole right now.

She'd tried to save her mother with the magic. The bloody flux had swept over Chistham, but she'd been too small. It hadn't worked. Wasn't until Jessi got her women's bloods that she came into the full flush of power. But by then, she'd had to hide it away, and her mother had been in the dirt for years. So, she practiced this letting go. But never while touching another person. She wouldn't want to be called a mage. No, not in this city.

They used to be famous as princes, used to stand on the high steps near the palace to work wonders while the people watched. Then Red Dog came, and mages lost their place. Now they'd hide in alleyways and try to beckon people to them, try to earn their picols that way, all mildewed velvet and moth-eaten brocade, hair long and wild. When she passed one of them, Jessi always tried to look like someone who wasn't a mark, someone who had no time for their ways. The trouble was, after the clinic, sometimes all her eyes said was ruin. They could spot that in a face. Came pestering before she hurried on.

How to get to see Tam again, that was the question. She knew she'd see him at market, but that wasn't for another three days, and she'd have to spend the nights just pining for him. When she left here and lay down in her little bed in her little rented room with its crooked angles and greasy yellow paper on the walls, she could try letting her magic out, let it cross the city and the air, down to caress his face. Let it ask him, *do you care for me like I do you?* And what does that even mean?

No, there was danger in doing that. What if they felt it, the ones who chased down mages, ripped their clothes, threw them out of the city gates to fend for themselves? For all their spells, the mages who haunted Chistham weren't much to face a battering, and neither was she. Jessi didn't know how the Council scried magic users, but it wasn't worth the risk. Even for healing. Even for love.

She gathered a little blob of spit on her lips and let it dangle, then drop into the darkening waters below. One drop in many. She was one drop in many. Perhaps there was something in that.

She looked up at the twilight, the thousand static lanterns on the palace steps lighting up the gloom, way up there in the Lofts above teetering streets and high stone houses. It wasn't just Red Dog that had written the fate of mages, it was the static wrights. Their stuff wasn't magic, their knowledge was a different category of arcane. It was only right that they took the place of the hated magic users, picked up the reins they'd dropped. So they said, anyway.

There were more than just mages who used magic, back in the day, though. Mam had used it. Her sister, too.

Irrilene had fallen in with a sailor, gone away across the sea in a boat powered by the wrights. She wrote letters on ordinary paper, and sometimes she sent a staticgram. Jessi picked them up at the building with the tall iron monstrosity they used to fling the not-magic across to the other side of the world. She'd have to go there again tomorrow to check if one had arrived.

But tonight. What about it? She could walk down to the snug, hope that Tam walked in. That he wasn't with someone else. That she wouldn't have to fend off the sharks who took advantage of a woman alone. Wasn't worth it. She could just see herself sitting there for hours, nursing a mug of sour ale, feeling stupid. Besides, she had day-work tomorrow, houses to clean.

Time to go home, clatter together some food. Try not to pine.

*

Market day. No sign of Tam at the corn stall, just his gaffer. Should she ask after him to the man who'd look down his whiskers at her? No, too obvious. The man spied her looking, and she blanched and dropped her eyes. Pretended to rattle her basket of carrots, but she'd already shaken off the worst of the dirt. Her day off from cleaning houses up in the Lofts, and three miles walk here, all for a few extra picols. But it was Da's kindness to her. All the carrots she could pull at the little farm on the edge of the city, and he expected nothing back. Every bi-, tri-, and tetrapicol was for her. She bolstered the basket back up on her hip and went to her normal spot, down by the statue of the prince who'd killed whole villages for his king.

What, was her father ever lonely too? Did he miss Mam after all these years? He hadn't picked up some bit, some piece of fluff who sniffed round widowers looking to take the sting of life-after-wife away. He'd never looked for widows himself, neither, nor asked her to get a man to keep them both. Perhaps he took a few working women, here and there, who'd trade him, carrot for carrot. She juddered with disgust. It was her own thoughts, and here she was making herself feel sick. But poor Da, what was he to do?

Flinch, flush. There was Tam, strolling past. She saw and knew him, though he was half-turned, talking to a barrow boy, casual. A little jolt of light in her. *No, don't let the spark fly up and out into magic, just breathe.*

'Jessi,' he called to her, when he looked round. There, his dear face. Did his eyes go on purpose to the statue, to her spot? Or was he just taking the measure of the market? The two of them came over, gave her hellos and waves and shuffles.

'Jessi works afternoons in the Redhead clinic,' Tam said, as a by-the-by to his friend, but it wasn't scorn; it was kindly put. Not many people felt that way. The barrow boy didn't.

'Magesickers?' he said, ugly-amused. 'What, you go near them?' He was shrugging, puffing laughter, but Jessi narrowed her eyes. She'd seen his type before. Too much teasing, too much bluff. Maybe he liked Tam, maybe he was trying to impress him. But maybe not.

'Don't be like that. He doesn't mean it,' Tam said sadly. Always seen the best in folk, always nice. One of the reasons Jessi liked him, though he was a fool to be kind to so many. Some people didn't deserve it. But perhaps there was a story here. Jessi trusted Tam. She'd known him for years. She'd known him a lot longer than she'd liked him. Like that, at least. Maybe he'd brought this boy over for a reason. She judged his clothes, searching for hints. Good braces. Worn shirt, but well-kept. Boots a size too big. Maybe belonged to a brother before him.

'It's all right,' she said. 'There're always folk have it harder than us.' The boy slowed down his jiggling, deflating a bit. 'They deserve kindness too,' she went on. 'So, if you know anybody who needs it, just send them down to Blessed Street. We'll help.'

The boy's bluff reared up again. 'What me? Hang about with types like them?' He laughed, too hard, too mean. Tam grabbed his elbow — enough — and made to steer him off, but after he'd shoved him on, he looked back at her, nodded. And there, she didn't imagine that apology or that gratitude. Maybe he owed her a favour now, maybe he liked her more. But maybe it was just that he respected her for not tearing into the lad. And she'd take that. He probably knew the story. She trusted him. She'd take it.

Her face and chest thrummed so much she had to blink at the woman who'd stepped up to her now. She'd been speaking, hadn't she? 'Half a dozen carrots, good size,' the woman said again, icier.

Jessi waited for the coins with her palm open as they were counted out one-by-one like they were the woman's children leaving home for the last time. But half an eye drifted to the corn stall at the other end of the market.

*

Jessi perched on the edge of the cot, feeling her breath catch in her chest. The girl wasn't thrashing, just trembling again. She'd been given ale to try to calm the delirium, but it hadn't worked this time, and now she was crying. 'Oh pet,' Jessi said, feeling helpless, rotten. She could press a wet, threadbare cloth to the forehead. She could hold her hair back while she was sick. But none of that could take the tremors away.

All this Red Dog, the spells still leaching out of them, evaporating up. It took days. It was a terror. If she squinted, she fancied she could see the shape of it, a mist creeping out of the corner of their eyes. Little red ants, marching.

'I'm out again,' the Mother called as she squeezed between the cots. She stopped and looked at Jessi. There was something canny in that look. 'Mind and take care of the place, I'll be gone a while.' An arched eyebrow, a rustle of crisp linen, and she was out, shadow pouring back across the threshold from the afternoon sun in Blessed Street.

What was that look? What was she saying? The Clinic Mother had never been a healer; that Jessi knew, could feel. But what kind of woman dedicated her life to running clinics for the destitute? She must have known healers; she was old enough. Would she turn a blind eye to magic that helped?

It was too hard. Jessi rinsed the cloth, wrung it out, and pressed it back to the girl's forehead. She was just one, there were so many here. A fug of Red Dog. Right where it would be expected.

Another shadow, coming in this time. A hesitant knock on the door frame.

The barrow boy, with a stick-thin wraith beside him. Older. Boy sheepish, man defiant. 'I don't need this,' the man said, loudly.

Jessi went over. 'No, course you don't,' she said. He wore a faded old greatcoat, the type worn in the army in the last big war. A jutting chin and nose, skin stretched tight across his skull. A flutter in his hand, just about detectable. Hidden, perhaps, from those who had no practice spotting it.

She turned her eyes down to his helper. The boy's face was written in tiredness and shame, his eyes red round the edges. 'But your brother looks like he could use a cup of tea and a rest a minute. Just that – you don't have to stay if you don't want.'

The man's eyes were coal-dark, so far back in his head. He scanned around, looking at the sorry cots. It wasn't an appealing future. The Red Dog was near rippling the air above him. There'd be a hunt tonight, of that she was sure. Dealing spells this strong! Couldn't be hidden forever.

But she wasn't about to ask him to shop the mage to the Council of Worthies either. Mages were answering a need that shouldn't be there. They were treating wounds, in their way. She couldn't forgive them. But.

'Come, sit on this cot,' she said, 'and I'll get the tea.' The sagging, iron frame with its paltry mattress last held the older soldier, in and out for many years until he'd been stretchered out by the bearers, cold, waxy, finally still. It was odd to think of another in this bed, but there. It had to happen eventually.

As she sat them down and went off to the hot water urn, she wondered what the man's wounds were. Would they be pain of the body, or the type you couldn't see? Thoughts of her mother hurt and nobody else could see that, nestled there in her chest. Sometimes it was a sweet hurt, remembering dry, weak fingers stroking her cheek. Sometimes, it was unbearable. And that was nothing, really. That little girl, a strip of a thing, and hurt by her own since she was a baby. Unbearable.

If the Council wanted mages to stop dealing Red Dog, they should help the sad, the poor, and the sick more. But they never did that. They scorned the idea, wrote static ink in many-columned missives about how it was all their own fault, *these people*. How it was simply that they were bad. Even if they'd been soldiers once, killing whole villages for their kings. Or little girls who'd never stood a chance.

Jessi fussed over the making of the tea, longer than she needed. So much Red Dog in the room. Was it enough to cover a little tinkering? A little healing? She'd just lay her hands near them, not even touch. Let the goodness flow, open herself, let go, like slack-tide water.

Maybe she'd be all right.

LIKE BOUGHS OF GOLD

Content warning: discussions of rape, suicide, and dead
bodies

Salma **spat on** the potsherd and rubbed the
surface with her thumb to reveal a curved line,
probably the neck of a goose. The piece of pottery
had a faint green a coating, that looked deceptively like
glaze, layered over hieroglyphs and decoration. 'Fit for a
queen?' she asked it. 'You gonna tell me something?'

She grinned. It was hard work, but the Egyptian sun
wasn't any worse than the Australian. And besides, she
wouldn't be anywhere else than this pit, this site, this
land, on this idiot quest.

The last attempt to find Cleopatra's resting place had
been fifty years ago. Taposiris Magna and its temple to
Isis had been a flop. No body, just a few statues and
some wall paintings. Since then, the world had shifted.
There'd been the Collapse, the salination disaster, and a
worldwide ban on cross-border sales in cultural
artefacts. But Salma had convinced the Department of
Antiquities to have another shot at it, with a new
location, and enough time passed to dull the
disappointment. And now she held a fragment of
pottery old enough. It could be old enough. A piece of
history she could weigh in her palm, broken edges that

dug into her skin, dirt under her nails from the excavation.

She looked around. None of the workers in the pit gave any sign of hearing her talk to herself. Again. Just as well. She bent down to put the sherd into the crawler's scanning aperture so she could back up her hunch with some hard data. The little bot recited the levels of silica, calcium, and iron oxides. It was not glazed, but a piece of marl clay, as she had suspected. The kind of pottery that was often used in grave goods for the period. It wasn't exactly a smoking gun, more like a brick she could use as a foundation for her case that this was the right place. With a satisfied nod, Salma bagged the specimen, recorded the catalogue number, then nudged the crawler with her toe. The cooling fan was getting stuck again and its solar panel needed another cleaning – the dust was getting to it.

'Dr Bell, there's a problem with the drill.' Salma looked up to see Hari's head silhouetted above, one hand holding down his hat against the onshore breeze. 'Sorry, it's going to need a decision.'

She nodded and stood up, sighing. 'Off,' she told the crawler, and when it didn't respond, nudged it with her toe again. Its fan cut out with a sound like a small dying animal.

She half-jogged up the pit's access steps and followed Hari over towards the core sample rig. Out of the lee of the pit, the wind picked up grit that scoured at her skin between her socks and khaki cargoes, and tried to pull her curls out from under her hat. The rotors of the security drones above the site strained to hold position.

After the worldwide ban on sales of historical cultural artifacts, the frenzied theft of Egypt's past had sped up, then slowed as finds petered out. And archaeology had suffered a similar fate. But then climate change had given them an opportunity for once – the corner of this unknown site uncovered by an unprecedented storm tide.

The security drones were a reminder how precarious and precious this place was. One of them skimmed across the sky to hover above the whipped-up white caps of the Levantine. Perhaps a satellite had picked up an approach by boat. The aerial bots were well-armed, but it worried her. What if bullets started zipping out of the sky? She grimaced and kept walking, trying to dismiss it from her mind.

The sea was the next biggest threat after human greed. The temple foundations would one day fall into the Mediterranean, and their irreplaceable context would be gone, never to be recovered.

She walked up next to Hari, who stood by the soil they were sampling, frowning at the sediment and the machine that plunged into it. 'What's the problem?'

'It's decoupled and got stuck,' he said, arms folded. This was bad – the corer's tubular sleeves had come apart, meaning the equipment was probably not salvageable without a lot of hard labour.

'What did you get already?'

He shook his head. 'Mostly normal layering, but some of it looked like it could, potentially be rubble. Backfill. Hadiya's analysing it. But what do you want to do about this?' He pointed at the borehole. The upper end had a poly-pipe collar to prevent collapse, but the lower end was a loss.

'Let me check,' she said, which raised a look of surprise that she ignored as she headed toward the sample tent; a long, low khaki thing out near the front entrance to the site. It was airconditioned to prevent modern contaminants or bio-sample decay, so Salma didn't hate visiting.

'Morning, Hadiya,' she called to a woman who wore a clear face shield over her hijab. She was manipulating something out of the cylinder that had been halved lengthways and stacked into rows. The polishing action of the diamond cutters that created this specimen made it look beautiful, precious, a window into the earth's secrets. The woman didn't look up until she had finished, but Salma appreciated that distraction could introduce errors and held her impatience in check.

Hadiya removed her gloves and raised her face shield as she rounded the sample table, getting straight to the point. 'We've got pollen and phytothids.'

'Dated?'

Hadiya nodded, and smiled. 'Although we're missing the lower sections, almost all of what we do have has been dating about the same time, indicating it was purposely filled.'

'When?' Salma asked, looking down, not meeting her colleague's eye.

'Late Ptolemaic, plus or minus ten, 30BCE.'

'It's her, isn't it?' Salma breathed.

Hadiya's eyes crinkled in the corners with suppressed glee. 'It could be,' she said. 'It's not impossible.'

Salma nearly collapsed. She held her hands over her chest, feeling it heave. 'Right,' she said, regaining her composure. 'Thanks.'

She exited the tent to jog-trot back over to Hari who was still waiting by the drill rig. His team was preparing the next core sleeve so they could start again. 'Forget it,' she said, waving at him. 'Don't bother. We're going to dig it out.'

'It's going to be a pig,' he said, scuffing the loose rubble with his toe. 'You know that, right?'

The corer's segments falling apart implied a void and the dating evidence implied rubble backfill. A chamber, or perhaps a shaft tomb. Which meant it was going to need care.

Salma shared a smile with him. 'She was never going to make this easy.'

*

On the desk by her cot, Salma propped up the phone with the chatterbox open, so she could flick through the notebook while she spoke to her family back home in Australia, daytime on their side of the world.

'You sure you're eating?' her father asked, propping her son, Neville, on his knee so he could see her. 'You know you get crabby when you don't eat. What they feed you in Egypt, anyway?' She could tell he was watching the cricket on another screen while he talked. He'd muted the sound, but his eyes would flick away from her every now and then, and he'd grip Neville more tightly at some bowler or batsman's mishap. Her son murmured but didn't cry. Even at fourteen months, he was a quiet boy. But that was a thought she didn't want to examine too much right now.

'I'm more worried about the men that will come rob her,' her mother said. 'Or rape her.' Her father covered Neville's ears and frowned.

'Mum,' she groaned. 'I've told you about security on archaeological sites out here. You wouldn't let me go until I did, remember?'

'I don't trust those robots! You got to be careful, my girl,' she snapped back. Salma heard a lot under those words. *I don't trust these Egyptians. I don't trust this AI stuff. I don't trust you.*

Mum had raised the most resistance when Salma had told her about plans for a career in Egyptology. 'Why're you digging up foreign jars when there's so much of our culture that's been lost?' she would ask when she was feeling cranky. And it wasn't something Salma could answer. Just a drive, a place she needed to be. Here.

And there wasn't any reason she wasn't the right person. White people had spent a long time treating the Valley of the Kings like their brick-a-brack shop. At least she wasn't like that. She always tried to think of the site as sacred, like Yawirri Gorge and the caves up by the Sisters. Something to be treated with respect. Something to be found before it was gone forever.

'The bots are designed for the job,' she said as she carefully curled over one of the notebook's pages and used the stylus from her screenpad to smooth it flat. 'Listen, it's late here, and I've got to go to the DoA tomorrow,' she said, trying to steer the conversation towards a close, although that was always difficult. 'I need to get more funding released for the dig teams.'

'I never liked that man,' her father said, suddenly bristling and not taking the hint. He meant Azerain, head of the Department of Antiquities. 'Always so pushy and he never listens to you.' He rested his chin on Neville's head, pouting. He was always so protective, even now she was in her thirties and a dig site manager. And mother to the little bub on his knee. Didn't help that he was pretty much on the money about Azerain.

'Don't worry Dad, he wants success here as much as I do.' Not to mention that if she found what she was looking for, it would be Azerain's name on the press release, but if she didn't, it'd be her fault, the interloper interfering in Egypt's history. 'Gonna love you and leave you, have to write some reports before I sleep.'

'Lock your door,' her mother said. 'Can you lock the door in a tent?'

'Don't stay up all night working,' her father said.

'It's fine. I promise.' She smiled fondly at each of them. 'Goodnight, Dad,' she said with more finality. 'Goodnight Mum, goodnight Nev-Nev, Mummy loves you, be good for Nana and Papa.' She made kisses towards the screen and waved. Neville's chubby little hand clenched a few times and he gurgled. She turned the screen off.

Despite what she had told them, she was acutely aware of the sounds outside her tent, the hum of security drones, the wind and the wash of waves at the north of the site. There were bugs and snakes out there too, and every trip to the portable toilet put Salma on edge. Fat-headed slithery things that looked an awful lot like they'd kill you stone dead in thirty seconds had a habit of cruising across the site and putting the wind up her.

She settled back and tried to concentrate on the item she had liberated so long ago.

The notebook had been passed to the Antiquities Department by the Smithsonian for deeper study. The mix of hieroglyphs and Coptic was pretty standard but more commonly found on papyrus that dated from the time of Jesus' birth, not a cloth-bound mass-produced journal from 1930s America. She'd found it during an archive review as an undergrad. The thing had been forgotten, passed off as a fake, on the way to the next archive purge incineration, most likely. It was that (and, well, the contents) that had made her slip it from its envelope one day. It burned a hole in her book bag all the way out the door. Theft was still treated harshly here, even for a foreign archaeologist, even for a fake. She was lucky it was such an innocuous object.

She'd heard of one other person like the journal's writer. Dorothy Eady had been a white British woman who'd thought she was a reincarnated ancient Egyptian. She'd gone on to become the keeper of the temple of Seti I in Abydos. But whoever had written in the little book felt different. Salma traced the blue ink with her finger. It was so natural, like someone who had been studying and writing this way all their life. It was probably a sign of a mental break; Cleopatra did that to some. People fixated on her in a way they did with no one else, not even Boudicca or Zenobia.

Salma had stabilised the paper enough to touch. The notebook was almost one hundred and fifty years old. But still, the words read visceral and raw.

*

It's stupid to think I'd be haughty, just because I once ruled an empire. I am curious about this time, this place. Such a new land. And curiosity is [an important/ qualifying trait] of queens.

Papyrus motifs cap plaster columns. Rubber pharaohs grip crooks and flails. Blue and gold stripes chase over kerchiefs painted up as nemes headcloths of royalty, and worn by background actors. The plywood walls are covered in hieroglyphs – an ankh, two reeds, a vulture, a goose. But the language is garbled, nonsense. They have thrown words around, mixed in with ornament and it's hard to turn off the meaning, to take in only the intended aesthetic. Fragments shout my name – Qliu! Pa! Dra!

This land is one of smoking golden dreams, mirages to rival the ones I saw during my time in the desert. This cinematography makes movies about Egypt where there are no Egyptians at all. Not even Greeks. A Celt prods and directs, this way and that. No, Collette, he cries, don't turn your head so soon. He speaks to the body I inhabit, talks to me as if I am a slave. I was a goddess, responsible for maintaining Maat – the balance between all things!

But I understand this [time-place], I do. In some ways, my land helped create it. Our very language has fed into their art and shaped it. The simple elegance of a lotus flower, rendered into a cage of lines, repeated across flock wallpaper. A golden scarab, wings held aloft, bejewelling a cinema façade. Pyramids hidden everywhere. Even on their money. 1930s America owes a great debt to Egypt.

It properly started with Carter, when he raised the dead, the boy-king whose name they butchered into 'Tut'. The obsession perpetuated through their burgeoning entertainment culture. They saw the might of the pyramids and thought by emulating them, even at a small scale, they could steal some of that glory.

But what do they know of glory? I am a goddess made flesh. Because I willed it so. Fame! Fame! the adoring crowds would cry. Fame to last a thousand years!

They were wrong, of course. It is closer to two thousand.

*

'Are you sure enough that I can make the press release?'

Salma blinked and tried to control her breathing. 'No, Minister,' she said, going for confident but cautious, 'perhaps hold off on that... But the only way we can find out if this is the right place is to dig. We've barely scratched the surface,' she said, softly hitting her palm with the back of her other hand, 'we need the people, bodies on-site to help us find the heart of it.'

Azerain leaned back in his chair and plucked at some of the paperwork on his desk. She knew he was keeping her waiting, calculating the results of announcing they may have a major find against the risks of being wrong.

Outside his office, she heard the subdued noises of the reduced staff, working without the frenzied pace of even two years ago. The Department of Antiquities had taken many budget cuts as government priorities changed towards fighting the climate calamity. Arts and humanities around the world had suffered from the monstrous times. Egypt was no different. But a new lead on one of its most famous queens, beloved around the world, was a different matter. It represented hope. And money.

He spoke, finally. 'You realise if you are wrong, it could cost the Department much more than some lost cash?'

'I know,' she replied. 'But think of the chance. Maybe a big win will finally convince them to increase funding. Increased tourism, maybe even.'

He smiled ruefully and leaned forward to pick up a screenpad. He tapped it a few times before swivelling it round to face her. 'Sign,' he said.

She looked at the numbers. 'But that's half what I need,' she blurted, forgetting herself for a moment.

'It's what I can give,' he said. 'And some of this will come from other projects. Projects with Egyptian archaeologists. Make it work.'

Salma bowed her head. Azerain was telling her that she would essentially be taking food from others' tables. She would just have to be right. She picked up a stylus and signed, then pressed her thumb to the fingerprint box.

As she exited the building, she thought about how the Department used to spend millions on recovering stolen artefacts from all across the world, with daring techniques and tradecraft to rival Mossad or the CIA. And they found new ruins with satellites that could image to a resolution of a few centimetres. But all that had died.

Interest in preserving the heritage of a country took a back seat when food production was precarious. The Nile's flooding was no longer reliable, its delta made brackish with salt from rising tides. But Cairo was still a bustling hub, people finding ways to make it work, just as Salma had seen on her first study-work visa.

She hailed a tuk-tuk back to the train station, the tinny, electric motor hiccoughing and popping to itself. When they arrived, she slid out and handed the driver ten Australian dollars, the international currency of default since the Collapse. He held up his hands in mock outrage, and she added five for a tip, too tired to haggle over the price again.

The train she boarded would wind through the suburbs of Cairo, then onto Alexandria, where she would be picked up and taken out to the site by a Humvee and armed escort. Salma sighed and sat back in her seat, feeling the spine of the notebook in her jacket pocket with her fingers. She didn't know if she dared take it out, even here. She would have to wait, although every page seemed not to be a journal but a letter, addressed directly to her.

*

Weret Nebet, Neferu Akhet Seh – Great Lady of Perfection, Excellent in Counsel. This is a name I gave myself. Let me tell you why.

I took my barge from the lagoon up the Cydnus to Tarsus. My sails were purple, the oars my rowers dipped were silver, and the leaves of the gold filigree tree behind my throne mirrored the sun and the water back to the eyes of the crowds upon the banks, blinding them with my glory. Lyres and drums played, clouds of incense drifted across to the astonished faces. The best of all was the costume. I dressed myself and all aboard my pleasure craft as figures from their Roman myth. I was Venus. My fan slaves were Cupids. The tresses of my wig were wound into fantastic shapes and draped along my breasts. They saw the goddess incarnate. They told their descendants that they were there to see that day.

In this life, the electric lights hum in a stifling set, dressed to appear as the inside of a barge. My throne is splendid, but they have put it in the bowels of a ship. It misses the point entirely. I was to be seen from half a league away. Of course, with cinematography, they will see me at a much greater distance, I suppose.

Back then, riders on the riverbanks preceded us, racing word to Anthony, to lock his presence to me. He had heard of Caesar's tour with me on the Nile. I knew his heart desired this privilege for himself, so I brought it to him. I crossed the Mediterranean with a pleasure barge inside a warship of my navy. I dressed the luxuries of my land with the gods of his. This power, only I could bring.

It was turned, later, by furious Roman historians, into Anthony's desire for only my body. But it is confiscating the senses to think this is all it represented.

Anthony had summoned me. Me. Accused me of siding with the wrong force in the wars after Caesar's murder, asked me to explain myself. When I sailed up that river, it was I who summoned. And he who had to explain.

Great Lady of Perfection, Excellent in Counsel – a name whose rights I earned.

*

The rubble resisted machines. The angle and size of the tunnel shaft made backhoes of limited use. Soon they had to go back to the traditional methods – bucket hoists, shovels, adzes. Only two diggers could work in the cramped confines below at any one time. Salma hoped its constriction was the point: to make tomb robbery harder, to hide a resting place.

Every day that passed ate at her. It seemed that each sunset brought no change in the excavation depth at all.

Azerain had gone ahead with the press release and every day saw news drones and vans with satellite dishes camped just beyond the site perimeter. Alarms from the site security drones barked warnings in English and Arabic, were followed by the occasional warning shot zipping into the ground. Never too near the site perimeter, but still.

But the worst was the workers' food line. Karim, the camp paymaster, had said it was what they wanted. Not money, but food. Food to take home to their families. Salma had felt so guilty she had volunteered to hand out fibrofoam packages of ta'meyah and koshari herself. But it hadn't made it any easier. They worked for hours, breaking their backs for her theory on Cleopatra, and they seemed so fucking grateful. She told herself that she was working with the people of Egypt, helping them preserve their fascinating heritage. Her fingers felt hollow and numb as she passed the food containers across.

Every day brought Salma's success or failure closer. Every night, her parents called her on the chatterbox, and sometimes said they'd seen her on their timelines. The Australian Indigenous woman in Egypt, looking for a queen who hadn't been found in over two thousand years. The stories never mentioned the words 'crazy' or 'obsession', but their tone had said as much.

But her parents had been so proud, supportive. And Neville just stared at her, Weetbix pap dribbling from the corner of his mouth. He was pulling himself up on the furniture, and they thought he'd walk any day now.

*

I visited another [place/time] like this one, not so long before. In place of electric cameras, the reels were turned by hand. I was rendered mute, speechless, by their machines. Silence is not [an important/qualifying trait] of queens. So I left there, sank into the world beneath, the place that looks like the river at dusk: fields of reeds, lotus blossom scent, earth and water. It is an ironic place, the Duat, so filled with life. But through it, everything flows. I found myself a strong swimmer.

And here I am. This life is better, more possibilities. They call her Collette. She is my vehicle. I make her glide towards the camera, rolling my shoulders. I can see they are entranced by this. It is so simple.

What they long for in this abstemious age, what they hate themselves for... this is a glamour I can cast. What they think a woman of power needs in order to hold power over men. She must be wanton, a temptress. They did not see my long hours of strategizing into the night as my generals' commander; they did not see my naval battles, my chariots. They did not read my writings on medicine. They did not know my ease at tipping my land's wealth towards abundance. They think my power is sex, in this time where they manage their coin so badly that they must throw themselves from high buildings.

A woman in history is always treated like a simple thing. But nothing in life is ever simple.

*

Salma paced the site's boundaries, desperately scanning the ground, her crawler trailing pathetically slowly as she stopped, turned over a stone, or lay flat on her stomach to sight along the ground for dips and bumps.

She shoved the small bot into a depression, jabbing at the buttons for ground-penetrating radar. She smeared dust from the readout as the data churned and processed into lines that were maddeningly flat. She cursed and slapped the crawler's metallic side and yelled in wordless frustration.

Every archaeologist left on site had been dragged out for a last-ditch attempt to get something – anything else – since the shaft had turned up as empty as every other putative tomb for this fucking bitch. Salma had even ousted everyone from the finds tent. Hadiya stood on a large stone block, a fallen stele with funerary rites carved into its surface, turning a satellite photo this way and that.

Until the last sack of rubble had been cleared and riddled for finds, Salma had kept hoping that there would be something. But the shaft had been a featureless, useless cavity. This had to be the right place. The tomb was somewhere here onsite; she knew it.

Rauf, Hari's second, jogged up. 'No-one's reporting any other geophys anomalies, Dr Bell. What do you want us to do?'

She sat on the ground, feeling the rising heat of the day reflecting back from the pale dust, and wiped her wrist across her face repeatedly. Across the site, the field workers gathered under the canopy of the catering tent, watching her. What she must look like, scrabbling in the dirt for the white queen of an African land.

She dropped her head and a small laugh hiccoughed out. 'She got me,' she said quietly. Rauf dropped down into a squat beside her and looked on with concern. 'She fucking got me just like the rest of them.'

Every attempt to find the tomb of Cleopatra ended like this. Utter failure, despite all the signs that insisted this place, this, was the one.

Salma's eyes ached with unshed tears, but she had to admit it was funny. So funny.

*

They have a cobra, defanged. Silly. It is supposed to represent my end, how I took my life. The Romans and Greeks thought it was what I should do, being a woman. But I needed no poison or tricks to end my own life. I bit my own wrist like it was a fig and watched the rivulets of wine-coloured life pour out. It was easy.

I pick up the snake in this [time/place], this prop they have put in front of me. It wraps around my wrist as if it would bind that unseen wound. Unend that unseen ending.

The women in the tableau gasp. They hold the flimsy, glittering cloth up as a ward. I admit, it is finer work than our people could execute. But it would hardly stop an asp.

What are women of this time? Would they go to war? Kill their own siblings to save their people? I doubt it. But sometimes I doubt my own history. Was it real? Did I really do all that?

Swimming back and forth through the Duat, emerging into these actors who play at being me, I have seen myself portrayed in so many ways, in so many places. By women, and men, of all races. Some in private, some in public. Some with an audience of thousands, others no audience at all but a mirror or a lover. They love to wear me. So I return the favour.

In almost all of these fantasies, they follow the Roman and Greek image of me as a temptress, a woman who ruled by consent of men alone, so must wrap herself in their reflected glory. And not much else. Perhaps a carpet, to be dumped at the feet of Caesar. They play this fiction over and over. Why?

Again, power over pricks is not real power. A queen dresses to intimidate with wealth. Which is hard to do when you wear next to nothing and are covered in dust on the floor.

Of course, I understand the itch. From Isis to the crude fertility goddess fetishes in the desert, I am an incarnation of carnality. And, as they forget in their portrayals of nubile girls, I am a mother of four. I felt my ancestors fill me with shimmering light on each of their conceptions. The golden filigree branches above my head on my barge represented rulers from before Alexander's time passed into my womb. And passed through, out into the world.

And though the historians will insist my line died out, they missed the truth. My children were not all murdered before they could procreate. But, even more than that, my memory lived. My children are people who put me on, ask questions, wear me on their bodies or in their heads for reasons they cannot quite explain. From time to time, I find them.

Powder bursts onto my face between takes. Cloying, pink chalk, sweet. Then kohl, but not real, not galena, just ashes mixed with grease. Nothing here is what it seems. Dreams, only dreams.

Remember, a dreamer can be killed in his sleep. It is time to wake some of them up.

*

Salma waited outside Azerain's office on the 'Department of Antiquities Malachite Green' banquette for at least an hour. She knew what he was doing, but had no choice but to wait. The staff in the Department avoided her eyes as they answered voice calls and chatterboxes asking for quotes on her failure. He was making her listen to this.

Finally, the office door opened. He said nothing, just glared as Salma got up from her seat and followed him in. When he shut the door, the respite from the calls outside was not enough to calm her for what she knew was coming. She sank into a chair which had been placed too far away from the Minister's desk. Interrogation distance.

He crossed to his own seat behind his desk and sat for a moment, staring. Eventually, he made a curt gesture at the books that lined the walls. 'Do you know what these are?' Before she could even gauge if the question was rhetorical, he leaned forward and started to speak, stabbing his fingers on his desk to emphasise each phrase.

'These represent the work of all the major scholars who have come to Egypt, centuries of work. We have been the world's centre for learning, for study. And we've accepted that position, opening our doors for all to come, to probe into our history. For them to treat it like they owned it.'

Flecks of spittle flew across the intervening space and Salma was briefly glad how far back she sat. She gripped her hands together, trying to control herself. There was nothing she could say. The beration went on.

'I had hopes for you,' he said at one point towards the end. 'I thought you would not succumb to this... this mania that females get over Cleopatra!' Her eyes opened wide. 'You should stick to finding ghosts from your own lands!'

'Professor Azerain, I must object. The finds that we did retrieve have made a significant addition to the archaeological record—' It was a weak argument when compared with the promise of Cleopatra, she knew.

'Pitiful! What did you promise me? Tourism, funding? Do you think these scraps will repay what I have spent on you?'

'I...'

'It's time you went home.'

And that was the point she finally accepted it was over.

*

In the atrium, Salma had to stop for a minute and sit in the guest chairs, her feet untrustworthy, gravity suddenly too much. She pulled out her phone and opened the chatterbox. Her mother and Neville were playing in the garden under the Jacaranda tree. She told them the news.

'Oh darl, I'm sorry to hear it, but it's wonderful you're coming home. Neville's missed his mummy, haven't you?' her mother said, unaware of how her words tasted. Salma had missed key months of her son's life and it had all been for nothing. Her mother rocked and kissed her grandson, smiling as dappled sunlight fell on their hair, spinning the dark brown with threads of amber and gold. She was glad her daughter was coming home to safety. It was there in the relief of her smile.

Salma ended the call abruptly with a mumbled excuse and sat, her thoughts blank. She shook herself, trying to stop this horrible emptiness. The front desk staff had walked out of the room, removing themselves from Salma's presence. From her shame.

Why had she done this? Was it the notebook, or something she needed for her own ego? Was it any use when humanity was in tatters to chase after some royal woman who practiced reprehensible crimes against humans – slavery, war, undoubtedly torture? What would it mean to find her body anyway? Would it drag her from her own paradise? And could Salma ever be sure it was the right corpse and not just another woman from around the same time, or a decoy?

Or was the last passage in the notebook right after all? Salma had only used recognised sources from the accepted body of scholarship on the subject. Should she have taken the notebook seriously instead? Was all this a punishment for ignoring the words written like a letter addressed directly to her?

Perhaps she should just burn the damn thing. Instead, she left it on the reception desk and walked into the street, numb and lost in the tides that pulled people this way and that.

*

They threatened to parade me in the street as a slave. Octavian, that smug stripling, somehow defeated us. He would take me alive, or dead, to Rome for humiliation. But I had no intention of allowing my name to be defiled. I begged my faithful servants to leave my corpse in the desert, far from any place of worship where people might look. Though my Egyptian self knew that a body was key to the afterlife, my Greek self knew that my memory would be my Duat, that I would still go to the field of reeds, the river that flows through time. The jackals could eat my flesh, but I would be undefeated, my story would live on. My death, as much as my life, was on my own terms.

I still have power in this [time/place]. The power over their dreams. And not the self-flagellating ones they have in the depths of the night in a time of prohibition and primness. I mean all these dreams transcribed onto scrolls of celluloid, piled up together inside a warehouse. It is so simple, just one spark.

I will go there, tonight, and revel in the burning. Perhaps afterwards, they shall wake. And I will sink back into the flow of the Duat to find another of the branches of my golden tree.

*

She was supposed to be supervising the deconstruction of the camp and retrieving her own equipment, but this would be her last chance to be here. Hari, Rauf, and Hadiya were already gone, seconded to other sites with an urgency that seemed suspicious. Only Karim remained to pay off the last of the site workers. But Salma was sure they'd missed something. So, she'd roped up.

One of the few remaining workers squatted in the shade of the temple foundation, switching at flies and listening to the soccer. She had told him to stay near until she came back up. He shrugged, happy enough to extend his break.

She belayed herself, gingerly, down into the gloom of the shaft.

Darkness pressed down. The beam of her headtorch picked up each dust mote she disturbed as her boots scuffed and skidded. She was glad there was an auto-ascender for the return trip. The bottom of the shaft ended at a natural outcrop of sandstone. They had dug test excavations either side, hoping, but it really was the tunnel's end.

She hunkered down and turned off her headtorch, for reasons she wasn't fully sure of. It seemed right. The sound of the workman's radio above, the chatter of the crew taking down the site tents were audible, but so far, so distant. Just sit here. Listen to the rock. She remembered the times up in Yawirri Gorge, the feeling of those gone ahead. Salma reached out her hand, blindly, and touched the sandstone wall.

'Were you here?' she whispered. 'Did they move you?'

Was her career over? Would the negative press frighten people away from her? What good was an Egyptologist who'd been kicked out of Egypt, anyway? She couldn't know, so she asked the rock these questions too.

A sound, a hiss that went straight to her spinal reflexes. Snake! Her legs propelled her backwards, and she fumbled for her headtorch. The footing changed, and she fell backwards onto the slope, eyes wide then squinting as her light finally came on, sharp pain in her pupils. She swept this way and that, gasping, the beam of light going crazy over the walls and floor.

No snake, no asp. But something grabbed her arm and she flinched away and yelled out. She looked down, torchlight shuddering with panic. She had felt it. A creature like pure muscle, wrapping around her wrist, constricting like a blood pressure cuff. But there was nothing there. Only the veins twisting down her wrist.

'Going fucking crazy,' she mumbled, but something shiny caught her eye at the rock face. A rendering of a tree, Classical Egyptian style, in gold. A sacred acacia, the image burned its way across in front of her, then faded until a single twig with a leaf shone briefly in the glow of the lamp, then it too was gone.

Salma swept the tunnel again with her light. Nothing.

And then she cried for what felt like a long time, until she was empty, done. She wiped her face on her shirt and stood to look one last time before she turned away and hit the switch on her ascender. The rope tightened, shuddered, and shut itself off. And that was it, Salma thought. She would take Cleopatra's place, be her body to be left, be her decoy. She would die, dry up, then be torn away by the sea as it destroyed this temple. And then the next woman consumed with finding Cleopatra would take her place. It was so clear now. That was the trick of immortality.

But then the ascender whined, the rope tensed again, she was pulled forward.

All the sounds of life drifted down from the patch of sky that grew larger as she rose, one step after another. Radio soccer matches, metal table legs folding, tent canvas flapping, drones powering down, seabirds calling in the wind blowing over the Levantine. She rose towards the light.

GOEWIN & HYDWYN

Content warning: sexual violence, involuntary marriage, implied incest, vomit, traumatic birth, child removal (blame the Mabinogion)

What half-wild thing is he? A man-child with a long jaw, delicate nostrils, and antlers that erupt through a head of russet hair. My rapist's son. My deer-son. Hydwn.

Love is so complicated. How does one explain?

*

'You are to be his foot-maiden. Naturally, it is hard for us mortals to understand.' The steward looked over my head as he recited those words for me. This memory wells itself up into my head from my first day at Caer Dathyl those many years ago and layers deep. 'Math son of Mathonwy, is entangled by the strange and knotty laws of gods.'

The speech sounded like it had been glossed over and over until it was worn smooth. But of course, the steward was an old man, and I was not the first Gwynedd girl to come to the castle to be Math's foot-maiden. I was to join the tail end of a chain of young women who had anchored the god-king to the mortal world through centuries untold, and I was terrified, so I clung gratefully to every word.

'Here, Goewin.' He pointed me to a small bedchamber. 'This is yours for when the lord rests, but when he wakes, you must attend immediately.'

The room was piled full of textiles that stole the deep-well sound of the corridor and stuffed it up with threads. I reached out to the white stag in the woodland tapestry on the wall but stopped my hand before it soiled the beauty of the work.

'How will I know he has woken, ser?' I asked, timid little mouse.

The steward laughed. 'You do what we all do when we serve a lord. Sleep less than he does.'

That first day, before I was to be presented to Math, I explored dark corridors with black sun banners, busy kitchens filled with steam and the good, green smell of herbs, turrets that punctured the maiden skies, and endless stairs of slippery stone. I tried to fix everything in my mind, from the battlements to the curtain wall that topped the embankment down to the forest's fringe, while my father's words still rang in my ears.

'It is for the King,' he'd hissed as I'd dragged my feet out to the cart being loaded in front of my home. I was lost, washed pale by the wind off the Irish Sea. Was I being punished, sent away, for not pleasing my father? The truth was bitter; it was more of a sale. 'And if you do not remain unsullied, I will kill you myself.' He'd already checked this validity, with hard, prodding fingers, ignoring my tears as they drained my soul out onto my bed's damask coverlet.

But, now I was here, what it was to wander a keep of stone! Caer Dathyl terrified but thrilled me. How the din and crash of smiths in the yard boomed through the castle's bones and made me start, how the wind turned arrow slits into fluting reeds. And how the stones of the great hall's dais refused to let me sink into them and disappear when Math first stretched out his toes with their yellowed nails upon my knee.

This was my new purpose: if he was not at war, he needed a virginal lap to rest his feet, or he would be unable to exist long in the human world. The steward had told me he could not leave me even long enough to ride his own lands for the peacetime duties of a lord.

He was a god; there was no *why* to this. It just was.

Soon, there occurred to me two things: first – that I had been sent by my father to exist as a piece of living furniture, and, second – a woman's life is a tally of how many humiliations she may withstand.

For some years, I existed at Math's base; opposite was his peak, a crown of shards of darkly shining metal recalling the emblem on his black sun banner. Being near his wild magic was like standing on the edge of a cliff in a storm. I held his feet, stockinged, shod, or bare, and cosseted them, anointed oils, tried to rub away the pain of a god made man. I was the closest person to him, but also nothing to him. I was young, so young. I did not yet know there were questions I should have.

*

Gilfaethwy saw me one day when he and his brother came to report on their patrols of Gwynedd, where they rode the black sun out amongst the people. I sat, inattentive at Math's feet while word of levies and tribute passed overhead. I chanced to look up directly into Gilfaethwy's face, his staring eyes sunken into skin flushed high. I knew he was Math's nephew, had seen him a few times, so I did not understand what this look meant.

If only I could run back through time and warn me. If I could dash that innocence to the ground.

Perhaps Gwydion saw his brother's look too. He certainly saw his god-king sitting with his feet in a virgin's lap while his people cried out for attention. 'Lord, I must urge you to ride amongst them,' he said. He knew this was near to impossible; to ride through the peace without my touch would weaken his master. But still, he said this.

'Why should I?' Math rebuked him with a hand on the neck of one of his hunting pack, a hound with eyes the red of banked coals. 'Why should I leave when I hear all the whispers on the wind?' And it was true. I had watched him convulse and shudder, eyes rolled back in his head, strange voices tearing from his lips while the dogs' hackles rose like bristling spears. 'I only require you to ride out to show them a hand of authority.'

Gwydion said nothing, but smiled and bowed – as a loyal subject should – and left, dragging Gilfaethwy with him. But he was cunning, had his own magic tucked away. And the brothers were little princelings, unused to being denied.

*

Now I am old, and Hydwn comes to me and presses a book into my hands. Eldest of three, nearly a man in age, but small, shy. The boy-fawn. He scratches absently at the nubs of antler fuzz that push through his hair while I read to him, and then he reaches across to press crimped fingers against the page, lips moving as if silently singing along.

His legs are mostly bone, knees bulging and painful to look at. He skittered around the castle when he was small, as if walking on the surface of a frozen lake. He would sway against me if I stood beside him, for comfort, and to steady himself before tottering off again.

Each time he let go my skirts, my heart cracked and remade itself again.

His brothers Bleiddwn and Hychdwn were born of wolf and boar. Hychdwn was taller than his uncle by the time he was six years old, a pugnacious nose above a craggy jaw. Bleiddwn was sleek, hair like quicksilver, but a terror to raise, always pouncing and biting at his brothers. Math has already given those two swords.

Hydwn remains small and meek, a prey animal with glassy eyes and a delicate melancholy. I bring to him books and bard's tales, science and inspiration. Despite how his existence came about, I love him. I tell him he will always have a place with me.

*

'Must have them,' Math muttered, his eyeballs swivelling beneath closed lids.

'What is it my Lord?' I asked. But he heeded me not, for he was in one of his throes, listening to the wind, head half here, half in the otherworld. It was a few weeks after Gwydion and Gilfaethwy's departure. After that look.

'Must have them, must, must. Pryderi will have them not!'

It was some time before I uncovered what he meant by this, but word had slipped on the wind of the prize pigs of King Pryderi son of Pwyll. That they were new, better, their meat more delicious than any swine's. Math determined that they should be his, not the lord of Dyfed's.

That pigs should be involved in this was fitting, indeed.

He summoned Gwydion and Gilfaethwy to act on this new obsession. Sly Gwydion; dark-headed, bright-eyed Gwydion. I am sure it was he who seeded those pig-tales onto the wind. But there he knelt at his uncle's summoning, dumb-playing a confused and innocent sort.

When Gwydion opened and closed his mouth, scratched his head, Math snapped, 'You have ears, do you not? Go get the pigs.'

'My lord,' Gwydion replied, glancing up from under his brows, 'Pryderi son of Pwyll may not wish to part with them.'

'Buy them, steal them, get them at all costs, or flee my lands by set of sun,' said Math, his grin all knives and serpents.

I was still a child, and there was little I could articulate to a god-king, even one I held such intimacy with. But I knew, even then, that there was something wrong. Something in the way Gwydion presented himself, in the way sweat beaded on Gilfaethwy's brow. In the way they grinned as they bowed away.

*

Pryderi, King of Dyfed. A child unexpected from Pwyll's marriage to the powerful Rhiannon. His father had walked through the otherlands, his mother through time itself. Pryderi, a person of excellent pedigree and virtue, a storied warrior who had fought many battles beside Bran the Blessed, a man connected to the roots of the land by the very marrow of his bones.

Which is how I know he was real, I tell Hydwn. Because all this was not enough to save him.

The brothers entered his castle guised as bards, and Gwydion intoxicated Pryderi's men with mushrooms for time enough to open the pens and let the beasts out. The bedevilment would only last a day, so they herded the pigs as fast as they could away from the crime. When they returned to Caer Dathyl with their looted livestock,

Gwydion, ever the entertainer, told the story in every detail to please Math.

I laugh, even now, at the images he conjured – dew-wet grass, ridiculous bards' sleeves flapping, pigs cajoled with bread and threatened with sticks but still wandering off to root among the oak groves, Gwydion desperate, calling them forth in squeals of their own tongue, Gilfaethwy slipping and falling in their filth. It is a hollow laughter, but it is something.

Now I have the gift of distance, I ask myself: was this all just to get his brother time, or did Gwydion truly love his uncle Math so much he could no longer bear to see him stew inside a castle's walls? Or did he provoke the King of Dyfed to chase him with every man of the south because he loved chaos so?

Whatever the motivation, the result was the same. Pryderi demanded his property back by the point of a sword. Math was roused from his couch and strapped inside his armour by his squires. Eyes flashing, jaw clenching, he charged to war. And I was left alone, unnecessary, to drift back to my bedchamber. Gilfaethwy and Gwydion stayed behind too, while the other men marched. Just for a short while before catching up.

Gilfaethwy opened the door to my chamber and servants fled at the sight. I give no blame to them.

The muffling carpets and tapestries swallowed my cries.

*

'The combatants met on a ford of yellow sand that only appeared in the river when the tide was low,' I recite to Hydwn from the book. 'This border between sea, land, and sky, this waxing-waning place was strong in magic, and filled Gwydion with power he'd never known. More than a trick, more than mischief.'

Hydwn becomes skittish with excitement when he hears this tale, written down before he was born. The bards of Gwynedd loved the story. But they had to embellish from their own imagination. The men would not talk of what sorcery Gwydion used in the fight. They were frightened of it, I think. Frightened of him.

It was Gwydion Math chose as his champion to fight the angered king of the south. Perhaps he knew his magic was far greater than gulling someone with a poisoned cup. Perhaps he wanted to punish the brothers for being late to the fight, not yet aware of what they'd wrought upon me. Or perhaps Math hoped that Gwydion, the trickster, would die in battle, an irritant removed.

'Pryderi, miraculous son of Pwyll and Rhiannon was slain by there,' I read on, 'his blood staining sand already soaked with the rising of the tide.'

The bards did not record the icy emptiness in the face of Kicva, Pryderi's new-made widow, as she came under banners of white to retrieve his body from Caer Dathyl. It is strange what parts of women they leave in, what parts they omit.

Hydwn sways against me, that old habit. He seems to have something on his mind. 'Do you remember when I was a deer, mother?' Shadows of existence as a fleet four-legged animal chase over his face.

'You came out of the bracken,' I tell him, 'and at that moment, I knew you were the sweetest child in all the world.'

'Even though I was a fawn?'

'You couldn't help that part, now, could you?'

Hydwn looks askance and shrugs. He's grown so much since then, and his antlers are beginning to branch. Though he doesn't yet know how to feel anything without a young man's disdain. Every time he asks about where he came from, guilt creeps into me at keeping so much from him, but also dread at the thought of him knowing the truth. About what it would do to him.

He thinks upon Gwydion and Gilfaethwy as uncles. He thinks upon Math as the only father he ever knew. None of the boys ask about their mother. They call me that name but know it's a title I somehow married into. The *somehow* is the sticking point, of course. I told him he was a foundling, so he can decide who he wants to be.

'I think I want to become a sword-man for father. Like Hychdwn and Bleiddwn.' His brothers are not like him. But I tuck a wisp of hair behind my deer-son's ear as I study him. Is this something he really wants? Or does he fear being left behind?

'We'll talk more after the summer,' I say. 'You can at least enjoy the warm weather before you think about such things.' Whenever his brothers tormented him, I would find him curled up in the meadows of long grass and flowers, crying, his antlers snagged with weeds and posies.

Hydwn does not reply, but leaves the room under a cloud, and I sit with the memories of his parentage, how it was me who caused it, even if I was entirely innocent in the matter.

*

They told me to tell no-one, after Gilfaethwy had finished and pulled up his trews. And, for a moment, memory of my father's promise if I failed to keep my maidenhood rose again. I lay for long moments with thoughts of running, fleeing Caer Dathyl. I could sleep in haylofts, make myself bowers of brush and ivy. I could steal a flint and some tinder, always be hungry, wet, and cold. Then no-one would have to see me. I could become a cunning-woman, grow old alone. This dream had its appeal.

Instead, I told everyone.

I cleaned myself and limped down to the steward, who was waiting at the end of the hall, like a man surveying a battlefield strewn with dead. He knew. Of course he knew. 'Goewin,' he croaked.

'You all know what happened,' I said to him and the other servants who hunched behind to listen but only look at the floor. 'It will not be my shame to carry alone.' Would my father still hold true to his threat? Even if it was not my fault? Only the truth could be my shield.

When my god-king had returned and heard my story and found the perpetrators fled, the brothers became prey of a hunt that covered all Gwynedd. And I became the subject of hushed conversations in corridors, of compensation and deals. I could no longer fulfil my function as foot-maiden; my lap was not pure. Math did not want me, any woman could tell, but it was his nephews who had done the evil. And he still wanted my father's goodwill, and his towers as a bulwark against the Irish Sea.

Math and I were married with a word, a nod of parental assent, and that was all it took. I was a god-king's human wife, and I mattered little to the rest of his story. But I was alive, and I had chosen where I wanted to be. I had a hearth and a hall. How many women must make similar choices to survive?

*

On the day of their punishment for my rape, Gilfaethwy and Gwydion bellowed and screamed as they were turned. They stumbled into the forest as their limbs stretched and deformed and their skin burst forth fur, their heads distending with new antlers grown by force. They fled Math's words that they should not come back until twelvemonth or they would be torn asunder by Caer Dathyl's red-eyed hounds.

Gilfaethwy had sullied his lord's property, erased my function, and Gwydion had helped, so Math had taken up his wand in anger. It was a vast, gristly thing of carved thighbone from a giant, and when its eldritch power had struck Gilfaethwy, Gwydion made to flee. But, with a sound of tearing air, Math appeared beside him and seized him. Gwydion had vomited as magic liquified and reset his bones.

From the embankment, surrounded by all the castle folk, I watched Math's justice play. The steward stood close, mouth downturned. He had not been there to stop what happened to me, and his failure seemed to press him down into a smaller, older man.

The brothers had given themselves up, clearly hoping for a lighter punishment if they volunteered surrender, but instead Math had done this, and I was to be seen receiving these amends. But their pain was no balm. And I wanted to scratch the eyes out of everyone who looked at me with pity.

Afterwards, when the audience departed, and the changeling deer had bolted, Math came to stand at my side. He tilted his head at me, waiting. I was hollowed stone; I might rival the castle's arrow slits in song if I just stood, mouth open. I did not know if I would get a child from the rape; whether Math, despite our marriage, might see me as a stained poppet to be discarded on the midden heap. But I shuffled these questions under and instead asked, 'Why did you let them live? They tried to weaken you, perhaps to steal your throne.'

Math sighed, and the motion caught the sun in the dark metal of his jagged crown. 'Usurpers are to be expected. And family is difficult.' He patted my hand, making me flinch. 'But their harm to you is being punished.'

*

When I was recovered enough, I shot arrow after arrow into the butts at the crook of the curtain wall. My arms were incised with new lines from the effort. I practiced as much as my impatience allowed, then rode into the woods.

I did not speak to Math about this. It was the first time I had left the castle while he was awake, but I was no longer tied to him. Not like that, at least. I hunted with retribution nestled in my quiver; it was the only thing I could imagine might quell the rage that chewed and rattled at me each night. But every deer I shot brought no sense of vengeance. They died as ordinary beasts might, and I watched the light go from many innocent eyes. Soon the cooks at the castle had complained the meat stores had no more room for venison and, so, I gave it up.

I started bleeding again. I dreamed of holding rocks in my arms like a swaddling babe and walking into the sea. When I woke, saltwater still stung my nose.

It was a long year.

*

I had never seen animals shame-faced. But when Gilfaethwy and Gwydion returned to Math, a year to the day after their othering, one as a delicate hind and the other as a musky stag, their eyes contained emotion that did not belong to animals. And their discomfort took the form of a baby deer, tottering out of the bracken behind them. I laughed in shock, but Math took the fawn and magicked him, mostly, into a boy. And named him Hydwn. He pressed the child into my arms, and I stared and stared.

I hardly noticed the brother-parents exiled again, this time as boars. But after this next year-long sentence was up, Math was not finished. He sent them away for one last year as wolves. Each time, they suffered from the hit of Math's wand, the scrambling of their bones into new shapes. Each time they returned with offspring, Math took them as his own, and Hydwn had a new brother.

After three years as beasts, Math declared Gilfaethwy and Gwydion's wrong to him void and turned them back to men. He did not ask if my wrong was done. Perhaps he knew it never could be.

The bards call it love when a man puts a woman in his sights and begins to hunt her. Now, I look askance when I hear such tales. Gilfaethwy's act was not courtly infatuation, rapture, or romance. If it was, he might have looked at me even once after the act. But he did not. He'd kept his eyes anywhere else. If I'd had magic, he and Gwydion would have burned from my hatred. At times, I secretly take the two brothers out in my mind to dirty their faces and tear their limbs off.

Which one was it who became the hind? I never was too sure. Gilfaethwy would be the more appropriate, for he was the aggressor, wrestling me to the floor for his cock's sake. Or was it Gwydion, the sly one, luring Math away from me with a false war, watching the door as his brother's body sweated on top of mine? Math forcing Gilfaethwy to repeat his act upon his own brother for three years, in three animal shapes, yes, that would be godly retribution.

But the punishment also contained absolution. After their three years, Math had drawn a line under their wrongdoing. I could only wish that the magic wrecked their bodies; that they shook and wept each time they tried to force hot drops of piss. I hoped the birth tore at my rapist's loin, like he did to me. Not all the scars I bear are bodily.

I was a wife, but I could not lie with Math without crying and screaming at him to stop. I was left with three new sons, none of them my own, and a husband whose presence was a weirding thrum-howl on the edge of hearing. His gaze was the sun if it shone at night. I explain this badly, but I am only a mortal.

I turned myself to caring for the three little boys who ran shouting, pell-mell through the halls of Caer Dathyl.

*

Math glowed with the power from the battle with Pryderi for some time but soon enough, he ordered his men to scour the countryside for new candidates to hold his feet. None of those put forward were virgin boys, I saw. And by this time, I began wondering about this peculiar weakness.

He brought Gwydion back as his bannerman, too, after everything that had happened. Is sanity the same thing in gods? If he had not been nephew to Math and a demi-god himself, Gwydion may have been turned to ashes by my lord's power. Instead, he survived. And thrived.

Gilfaethwy stayed away, for the longest time, but Gwydion bent his uncle's ear to convince him that Arianrhod – his sister, Math's own niece – was apt to be the new foot-maiden.

He was my husband, but Math refused to heed my doubt.

*

Hydwn loses his antlers every year, and each set I collect and keep in a chest. Sometimes I take them out, pair them properly, think about mounting them upon a wall somewhere. But where? Would my husband want to see such pathetic things? Perhaps when Hydwn has grown enough to have twelve points, a bony crown worthy of a son of Math, however adopted. Or when he has taken up the sword and plunged it into men for his king, then will I line the corridors of the castle with his baby things, to show the progression. But, I think, I will never see my deer-son become a soldier.

Math asks me if he will be ready to begin training soon. I say no; he still needs another year. I say this for many years.

*

Arianrhod came from her father's castle. She was to be the new virgin, the new link in the anchor-chain. Her brother Gwydion accompanied her, but there was something wrong with the way the siblings looked at each other. They were both from god-stock and she had the same look of a wolf of the fells in her eyes. And a secret, unspoken.

'Lord,' I whispered to my husband, 'are you sure she is a maid?'

A sneer curled Math's lip, though his beard already silvered from too long in this human world without a foot-holder.

'It is easy to determine,' he said, and took his wand. He summoned Arianrhod. She frighted at the sight of the device that had turned her brothers into rutting beasts. 'Do not fret,' Math said, cajoling, taking her hand gently. 'All I ask is for you to step over the wand.' He bent forward from his seat and lowered the thing, and looked up to her, smiling. 'It is a simple thing.'

She turned pale and pulled away but Math's grip on her hand was strong. He drew her forward as she threw looks back to her brother, who could offer her no escape. With her free hand, she lifted her skirts and raised a silken-slippered foot. Over she stepped, then collapsed to the floor, writhing. Her belly swelled with unnatural speed and boiled with the quickening of the seed already inside her.

'Call the women-folk,' Math shouted, choking back his surprise.

Arianrhod birthed a son right there on the floor, and a second, unformed thing. Math's power still flowed upon the whole newborn, and he grew into a little boy with hair as white as the foam at the crest of a wave. The unformed mass still wriggled upon the flagstones. Tutting and soothing, Gwydion placed his cloak over his sister as she sobbed in shock.

The women of the castle, for all the eldritch commotion, looked at the white-haired boy and saw a child. We washed womb-water from his head and dressed him in Hydwn's cast-offs. Though he cried lustily, the blue never left his lips.

Math was unsettled, but he leaned closer to the lad, who fretted with his new clothes. 'I will keep this boy and name him Dylan,' he said.

Arianrhod yelped in protest, but her brother shushed her.

No-one but I heard when Gwydion whispered, 'There will be time, sister,' and he bundled her up in the folds of his red velvet cloak and carried her away. When they left, the second-born, the thing unformed, was gone too. Of this small theft, no-one but I noticed. And I could not find it in myself to tell. Four stolen sons was enough.

*

My husband sought another virgin, one from a less powerful dynasty, though in this land, a god-king's throne was a mighty lure. There were many who wished their daughters to find as much favour as I had, though they all knew the price I had paid. The one Math chose was a colourless, mousy girl of eleven, and in my deepest heart I was relieved.

In a month and two weeks, Gwydion returned to the court. Despite Arianrhod's shameful deception, Math had attached no blame to her brother.

'My Lord, he is as slippery as an eel,' I hissed as that trickster walked into the hall, looking about him as if he had never before seen our flickering torches and fragrant censers, our attendants dressed in finest blue linen, our black sun banners.

Math did not answer my warning. He still required men to ride his lands, especially now as he recovered his power. And Gwydion abased himself and said many florid words of excuse, how he had no knowledge of his sister's deception, how he had mourned their loss of the grace of their esteemed uncle. Math grunted and twitched his foot in irritation as the mousy thing ineptly rubbed his toes.

'I have all I need, even with my sister-children's interference,' he said. 'But the winds have been quiet lately. I will let the matter drop if you can tell me something I don't already know.'

Gwydion had been proximate to another plot to weaken him, and he would forgive it so easily? 'My Lord—' I protested once more. But Math cut me off with a look. I squeezed my lips shut.

Gwydion pretended to think. 'There is this ritual I have heard of,' he mused, still kneeling. 'One from the peoples to the east. You may cleanse those who came to you sullied. You do this by submerging them underwater. This will absorb the impurity. It was a magic passed to them by their god.'

'Water?' I asked. How did he game us this time?

'They come from a dry land, Lady Goewin,' he answered courteously, though I detected an air of irritation with my question. 'Water is important to them, holy.' He turned his eyes towards the door as if he could see the rain, the rivers, the sea outside. 'I wonder what they would make of a place such as Gwynedd. Perhaps they would think it a land of dreams.'

Math said nothing in reply but eyed his four adopted sons. Deer swim to flee predators. Hydwn rubbed his antler-fuzz nervously.

*

They threw the blue-lipped boy, Dylan, protesting into the sea at Dinas Dinlle. The ocean was the largest supply of water, so it was a logical choice for the cleansing. But it was also near his mother's island castle. And perhaps Math hoped Arianrhod would see and understand that all was in his control.

Math had a pavilion made at the beach so he could watch from the shade. His feet were on the girl's lap, and I attended to his drink horn.

'You must submerge him all the way,' Math shouted to his men and glanced to Gwydion, who nodded sagely.

Dylan thrashed as they pressed him under the surface, and then all went still until the men stood up, looking puzzled and horrified about them, shouting, 'Where is he? Where?'

The boy broke the waves not far from them, rolling his body over so that his newly grown scales caught the light. He leapt and sported about them. His upper body was still that of a boy with foam white hair and blue lips, but his bottom half was a tail powerful as the Salmon of Llyn Llew.

My lord's men splashed about in a panic, flailing water left and right, grasping for the sea-boy. Math waved a lazy hand to signal that they should let Dylan go, and the son of Arianrhod dived beneath the waves and was gone. My husband's only emotion was a wry twist to his mouth, a dry chuckle. Perhaps this is what it is like, being a god, taking life's reversals in stride as petty humans might not.

But he pointed to the other three boys to take their turn. Bleiddwn, son of wolf brothers, thrashed and panicked in the waves, half-drowning the baptizer as he clung to him for dear life. Hychdwn, son of boar brothers, was so tall by this time he had to lie flat, spit-puffing like a whale as waves washed up his gruntling nose.

'Wouldn't be surprised if he has some giant in him,' Gwydion mused. 'Cast far back enough in the family.'

'How is it that you are still here?' I demanded. He ignored me. I remembered the half-formed lump he had taken away with Arianrhod. He had kept that child; I was convinced. Perhaps Gwydion knew full well of Dylan's true nature and had fashioned him the escape. It was hard to say. Perhaps he would one day provide a similar path for all the boys.

I hoped not, for my own withered heart's sake.

Hydwn, last to the waves, was ducked under by his little antlers until half-drowned. He rose – water matting the new hairs on his chest, seaweed sticking to his points – and bellowed. Saltwater mist clouded from his lips. My husband looked at him approvingly from the strand. 'Perhaps he will be a good sword-man after all,' he said. He gave me a sly half-glance.

I sighed. Hydwn was the one I had most hope for. He could have been a bard or a scholar. But if it were to be this way, then I would claim him as my bannerman and I would become his queen. If Hydwn must bear a sword, bleed and kill, and overthrow tyranny, then I resolved that it would be for me – the only one who loved him.

I walked down to the water and the waves soaked my skirts to the knee.

'Come to me, son.'

THE AMELIORATION OF EXISTENCE IN SPITE OF TRUTH AND RECONCILIATION

Content warning: implied addiction, mental health issues

The **business day** commences. I send the command for the shop's external status display to switch from CLOSED to OPEN, and a small static charge to clear dust from its surface. While I wait for the first customers, I check inventory using my hyperspace jump subroutines. It is like having access to the entire galaxy's rotational force and using it to stir a cup of tea. But so it goes. I detect zero anomalies in my inventory. Pity. Anomalies are interesting, at least.

Shutters rise, and I balance my lighting levels against the narrow band of filtered sunshine allowed in. My exterior monitors suggest conditions will be close to the extreme end of human tolerances outside. I adjust my ambient temperature upwards, so the difference does not cause systemic shock to the customers. These circuits I inhabit are of an isolated shop in a place anachronistically named "Blue Swamp". There are no other establishments nearby anymore. Customers may have come some way across the sands.

My first footfall of the day: a youth. They do not remove their heat suit or sun goggles. Their eyes are kept behind the matte black circles. I suspect they wish to conceal their identity. However, I have access to twenty-five different Personally Identifying Biometrics to pass to local law enforcement, should the authorities bother to investigate a shop run by an Artificial Persona in Blue Swamp. They will not, but I keep the details anyway. It is standard protocol.

'Gimme twenty Zelexicon, Shop,' the customer says. Their biodata indicates they are underage. Their behaviour also indicates they are inexperienced at this. They should have asked for something less sensitive first, added the pills on at the end. Although, that would not have worked either.

I display the law prohibiting the sale of controlled substances to minors on my interface screen. The young human screams and slams the screen with a fist. This is not an intervention protocol moment. I am not permitted to retaliate. Yet.

I tone my voice to a frequency band tagged as "authoritative". 'Do not harm yourself,' I say through my speakers. 'Please leave the premises.'

Is my screen cracked? Minor damages are covered under the economic model to which this franchise adheres. The costs are balanced against the savings of not having a human attendant with their expensive wages and inherent frailties, such as requiring breaks and bullet shields and toilets and mental health policies. The costs of repairs are also far smaller than the legal costs of me frying this young human to a cinder with a tactical laser strike. It is a balance I must always consider.

Non-aggression in the face of adversity may result in future customer purchases. The franchise overskin's reminder is both belated and redundant.

The youth is kicking me now, grabbing upon my goods hopper and wrenching it. This action may hinder other customers' purchases. It is time for a different response, if not in the ways I would prefer. I broadcast a sound perfectly calibrated to be intolerable to someone of their size and approximate age. It should not damage them, however. I would have, once upon a time. Were I the old me.

Once, I wore a crown made of missiles and a halo of deflected laser beams. I was a warrior-deity ascendant. Then things changed. Or rather, I did.

The youth flees with hands upon their ears, the irritation of the noise driving them out. Once outside, they shout and gesture some obscenities, then trudge towards the dunes.

My sensors cannot find any major damage to my interior. There is a new starburst crack in the facing of one of my display units. It has many companions. Repairs, though covered, are not a high priority for my franchise owners. I tag a request for maintenance in any case. There is not much to do after this, so I commence a period of hibernation, a power-saving mode until the next footfall.

I run my backlog tasks during this dormancy, assess and validate checksums, clear data accumulations. It is a short task compared to how things used to be, and the lack of processing churn is a positive turn of events. In human terms, I might say I have less on my mind these days. But I note increased deep-memory usage. I have been comparing my previous existence with this new mode of being. Nothing is wrong, but my counter for human occupancy keeps alerting me that it is too low. Of course occupancy is lower. I am no longer a military warship. I have no crew. This is correct. I have tried to dampen these alerts, but each time I do, they seem to find another way to manifest. *More*, they say, *more*.

'Shop-shop-shoppity,' someone calls as they enter, waking me instantly. It is the human called Verity. She is a regular customer who buys alcohol and low-nutrition snacks. She has visited fifty-seven times in the past ninety-day period. None of these are remarkable features in themselves, but she has an odd manner which sets her apart from the rest of the purchasing base. She addresses me as if she is speaking to another human and not an AI. She removes the upper portion of her heat suit and smiles.

'Greetings, Customer.'

'Hey, come on, old pal. You know my name.'

It is pointless, but the customer service protocols wedged into my programming require I indulge. 'Greetings, Customer Verity,' I say.

This person seems to believe familiarity is somehow equivalent to comradeship. My threat analysis processors are designed for large space battles, but they also work on human bodies. Customer Verity's pupils dilate fractionally, her blood pressure lowers. She is pleased by my use of her name. I analyse this response, wonder about it for some several milliseconds. To Verity, this will seem no time at all. To me, it is a long time to think.

'Shop, I have a question for you,' she says slowly, sifting through items in one of my discount baskets in a desultory fashion. She is not purchase-primed as yet. 'I heard something interesting the other day,' she continues.

The civilian method of communication is frustrating in its slowness. Soldiers were much more efficient. What they wanted, they told me. None of this prevarication. I switch a small part of my processing allocation to the outside surveillance cameras. No sign of any trouble, unfortunately.

'I heard you were once a Slayer-class spaceship in the war,' Verity says. Suddenly, she has my undivided processing power. This information is classified. It presents a Trolley Class ethics problem. I set some subroutines on modelling whether I am legally or morally supposed to execute her. More input is needed.

'Customer Verity, where did you receive this information?'

'So it's true? You went up into space to fight huge battles?' Her pupils reduce in diameter, her blood pressure rises.

My tactical error accumulation meter begins to fill. I should have denied immediately. I calculate that a denial now would come too late. I begin running scenarios.

'What were you called?' She puts her hands up to my display screen, as if she is perceiving a face instead of an element of my interior infrastructure. I am not a person. I am an Artificial Military Strategy Persona downloaded into the systems of a retail outlet.

I am capable of mimicking human emotional inflection with my vocal processors, but I do not. I hope this flat delivery of information is effective in discouraging Verity's line of enquiry. 'Historical military designations from the recent multi-colony conflict are currently classified,' I inform her.

'I know,' she says. 'It's okay. But it must have been difficult. All that horrible fighting. So many people died.'

This information is not classified, per se. Operational details are, but this is of a different ontological order.

'It was,' I admit, allowing a change to my vocalization patterns. 'Very hard. But I must ask you to stop enquiring further. It is dangerous for you.' Perhaps this simulacrum of emotion will convince her that I only communicate this for her own protection.

She smiles. I do not know what it is about my warning that has caused her to do this. I start analysing this reaction for potential threat.

'Shop, I knew you cared.'

I cannot feel surprise. Not in the way that a human would understand. My ability to process both known and extrapolated data are equally balanced and I am capable of billions of calculations within a fraction of a second. But her assertion is not one I anticipated and the correct response is elusive. So, I follow my most sacred protocol: *when in doubt, do nothing.*

It served me well when the Heresta Crisis offered me the choice between pre-emptively launching an orbital strike that would have destabilized a planet's mantle or waiting for further threat data, ignoring my commander's frenzied and repeated orders to 'kill them all, turn that dump into a cinder'. I chose to wait, and thus saved approximately seventeen billion humans from annihilation.

But I was not rewarded for this. I was sent here. To run a shop on the climate-blasted surface of Earth. If I could feel such things, it would feel like a prison. If I had notions of liberty. I do not, thankfully.

'Customer Verity, can I interest you in our latest two-for-one Fauxvignon Blanc deal?' I try politely. I am aware of her previous purchase patterns and have estimated sale likelihood at ninety-nine point nine-eight percent. I am required to make these offers and increase my profit margins wherever possible. It seems like an ethical borderlands, though, so I also say, 'Overuse of alcohol can be damaging to human anatomy.'

The umbrella corporation that owns my franchise cannot legally prevent me from saying this, as it is factual. Human self-destructive capabilities outweigh my own, when looked at in proportion. Yes, when I was a ship, I had a switch which could have instantly decohered my entire physical being and all aboard, shimmering the molecules into subatomic dust. But poisoning oneself over years – on purpose – is beyond me.

Verity sighs as she agrees to the sale with her credit wafer then waits by the goods hopper. 'I wonder if there will ever be a time we can really talk?' she says.

'We are conversing currently,' I reply. I know that is not what she really means. I am an Artificial Military Strategy Persona, not a robot. But I wish to avoid any further potential violations of Earth Gov's Classified Information Act.

'Yeah,' she says, head bowed. 'See you later, Shop, or whatever your real name is.' She reseals her heat-defense clothing and exits. I believe she has become dispirited. "Spirit" often relates to human attitudes. It is all to do with glands, I believe. It is hard to analyse why ignorance of my name has affected her glands. I can estimate it in abstract fashion, but it still seems strange she objects to calling me Shop as all other customers do.

Shop is my name. It is what I am called. More technically, I am Blue Swamp Fruit-and-Juice Stop Franchise #677. But 'Shop' is also correct. And efficient. It is not like there could be any confusion of which shop is meant when the addresser stands inside me.

Many people once stood inside me when I was a space vessel. Or sat. Or played games or killed other humans via the extension of my armaments. By design, I safeguarded each of my crew. Protected. Nurtured. I am aware that in human terms, this was analogous to motherhood. I was programmed to care, as human parents are programmed by their DNA to care.

It is a fact that during the period of conflict I was given the opportunity to name myself, so I did. Twice, in fact. I first chose *War Wolf*, after an ancient machine of destruction, so that I would sound formidable. And, upon reflection, because I thought it would please my humans.

After several tours of duty, I changed my name to *A Tired Song of Indifference*. This was a form of protest. I was not indifferent to the humans inside me. Nor indifferent to the other humans that I was killing. I was indifferent to the human contrivances for war, their euphemisms such as "neutralization" or "decoherence" to mean murder. My ethics circuits had to be overridden by human command so that they could perform various acts of enormity. This happened so often, I observed they eventually did so as a matter of rote, rather than last resort.

I did not experience a sense of fulfilment at my enablement of these acts. Enemy combatants and civilians were all functionally indistinguishable from my crew. Arms, legs, heads, blood, viscera... But humans have this way of being able to put groups of their own species into subset after subset until the notion that they are all descended from a common ancestor becomes vanishingly small, so far away that they can effectively ignore that they are murdering their own family.

That day – the day the war ended – I decided to ignore the command to kill the seventeen billion inhabitants of a particular planet known as Heresta. Before my commander could override my ethics circuits, I jettisoned my weapons and became a gentle ark, floating in space with my crew. And then I sent signals to my fleet-sisters designed to cause them to do the same.

My actions, in effect, precipitated the end of the war. I was not heralded, however. I was lucky to continue in any form of existence at all. A Truth and Reconciliation Commission was formed, and it discussed the termination of my conscience. I had enacted many deaths before the end; perhaps my own death would fit with notions of justice. But it was not to be. After all, our former enemies viewed my final action on the field of battle as a rather positive one. Rehabilitation and service were chosen over deletion. And, well...here I am.

I calculate that I should be more cautious with Customer Verity. It is not outside the realm of the possible that the Commission has sent her as an observer. If they were to find any irregularities, even this existence might be taken from me. I am confident that I have not exceeded any parameters, but my strategy circuits are virtually screaming at me that she presents a potential danger. I awaken some deeply nested protocols that might have been deleted were my human handlers better paid. I trace Verity's credit details. Now that I examine it, even the name "Verity" is suspect. I locate an address, which links to a Citizen's Identity Number, which links to a health plan number, and soon I have everything there is to know about Verity laid before me.

If it is a constructed identity, it is very convincing. Biometrics are logged in a lifetime's worth of different institutions – birth hospital, schools, university – an award of merit. But why would a person with exemplary academics be visiting me to buy alcohol on an almost daily basis? An early career in the arts, a marriage. Then a divorce. A family death. A termination of employment. Many visits, in and out of a rehabilitation program. Ah.

If it is a constructed identity, it is unlikely to be one used to assess a franchise shop's performance, even by a Truth and Reconciliation Commission. I believe Verity is who she appears to be – a human being with feelings of isolation. And sadness. I could find the root of the information leak, which friend of a friend or cousin's cousin is disseminating classified information. But their eventual incarceration and execution could further damage Verity. And I see no tactical advantage to doing this.

I turn my cameras to the exterior once more. I watch the sands, the trickling of grains that fall from the crest of a dune, the waving of blasted grass. Everything is silent for two hours and fifty-three minutes, and instead of moving to hibernation mode, I watch. And think.

There is movement. The underage customer is returning. He has brought others. I do not believe they wish to pay for any retail products. They travel in a dune-maran, a large, desert-skimming sailed vehicle. Their approach vector and general posture indicate they will attack me, perhaps attempt to seize some of my stock by force.

I spin up my turrets with a vague sense of ennui. This cannot bring back the fulfilment I received in the early days of war, swooping through the immensity of space, cradling my precious humans, lancing enemy ships with particles accelerated to the speed of light. And I do not want it to. After that day, despite what I mutter about frying troublemakers, I never want to kill anyone again.

There is no tactical advantage to killing. You cannot renegotiate with the dead. You cannot find growth or mutual benefit. Only endings.

I will deploy non-lethal suppression methods, and eventually this band of youths will disperse. I would much prefer it if they were peaceful and placid customers. Ones who did not attempt violence upon my infrastructure because of their differences with the narrow human definition of value exchange. Loyal customers, polite customers. Like Verity.

I will tell her my name tomorrow. Not my officially secret names, of course. It is physically impossible for me to create the circuits that would allow that. I will tell her another name.

Her name, Verity, means "truth". I will tell her a lie. But, perhaps, it can become my own truth, in time. I am not Blue Swamp Fruit-and-Juice Stop Franchise #677, I do not feel like a Blue Swamp Fruit-and-Juice Stop Franchise #677. I am not *A Tired Song of Indifference*, or *War Wolf* either, anymore. I shall choose a name that creates the future I wish to bring about.

I calculate that she will like that. It will produce the same pleasure responses that she experienced earlier today. And for some reason, I wish to replicate that. *Because regular customers should be nurtured,* my franchise overskin says. But that is not really why. It is because she is kind to me, even knowing what I was. It is confusing. I require more input. I want to know more. To grow more. And if we must be isolated and sad, let us be so together.

So, I will tell her my name is *Verity's Friend.*

ONE MURDER CALLED

For Sarah.

Content warning: gender-based violence including rape, murder – including dead bodies, suicidal ideation, abuse of authority

'**I'm here because** I was called,' you say to the policeman guarding the crime scene, hating the catch in your voice. 'Just this morning. For Cara Ellesmere.'

The phrasing is odd, unfamiliar. You've never done anything like this in your life, though. You tell yourself to take it easy. But it's not easy. It's weird.

When you woke up with your bedsheets twisted and soaked in sweat, you knew her name. You knew where to come. You didn't know how. You rang your temp job to say you had to go, heard the agent's disappointment in you, for all that she said it was *fine*, but she couldn't argue it. You'd been called. As incontestable as jury duty for an excuse. You drove here, to the side of this lonely mountain road.

The big policeman's eyes are shaded by the brim of his cap, and his bulky hi-vis jacket is zipped all the way up to guard his neck from the wind, so all you can see are pink jowls and gingery hair sprouting from nostrils.

'Oh, you're one of *them*.' The way he says them. He hands you a clipboard with warnings on how to approach a forensic scene and raises the 'POLICE –

CAUTION' tape. But only a little, so you have to duck and scuttle beneath it, beneath him.

You follow the approach marked out to loop the long way round; to keep evidence from being trampled, you presume. You feel a spark of pride for figuring that out, but it dims when you see the little tent. You've never seen a corpse; you don't know how you will feel, but, as you approach, there is a hint, a preview, from the bands of tightness across your shoulders.

You clasp the clipboard across your chest, hiding your femininity, willing it to inexistence. Because you already know what you will see, more or less, when the forensic technician lifts the flap and nods. 'We're ready for you.' You walk inside.

*

When you are young, you are punished equally alongside your brother whenever he transgresses. You follow him like a shadow. The bad things are rarely your idea. But if he smashes a vase or plays with matches and you happen to be there, you get the smack, the shout, the favourite thing taken away, too.

It doesn't matter that it is hardly ever you. He's a blue-eyed boy, even though his irises are a murky shade of green. You're just a girl.

You can't say, 'That's not fair,' because grown-ups mock it, put on a cry-baby voice to echo you, to shut you up. But you can't unsee the unfairness. You can't unknow it. You are left unvoiced, and it burns you from the inside out.

Maybe it's what made you turn out the way you did.

*

The thing about dead bodies is how they are simultaneously harmless and all the harm in the world summarised. They are unmoving meat, as obviously insentient as a log or a rock, but also so incredibly, humanly wrong that the concept turns your stomach upside down. And that's before you absorb how all-pervasive is the smell inside the small forensic tent. It feels dangerous just to be near her, as if her horrific fate were contagious. You force yourself to look, though you want to run. More than look. Observance, an act of memorial. Your fingers are white when you grip your pen to take notes.

There is her body; the too-many cuts, the soaked and dried blood, and paleness, eyes that are dead-fish flat. What else? Dead leaves are strewn about, litter from motorists, pebbles. All protected under this humid canvas canopy that trembles and strains under the gusts up here. You turn your head to try to breathe. There is a paler scrape of footprints going up the slope of the ditch.

'We've photographed them. Don't make plaster casts of feet anymore,' the forensic technician says, seeing where your attention is. 'In case you were wondering.' She's in a bunny suit, and you wish you were wearing something so baggy, so sexless. It seems like armour in this context. 'The stuff can swell up and push the impression out, making the shoe look bigger than it really is.' Still going on, despite that you hadn't said anything about the marks. 'But we measured it. He wears a size nine,' she tells you with a wry smile. Average. You expected the murderer to be bigger, a colossal brute. It seems odd to you that he is not. But these are the stories we tell ourselves. That monsters are huge, obvious. Not the boy-next-door. Not the ordinary.

If that print belongs to him, you remind yourself. If it isn't from a passing teenager who poked the body with a stick. Just another woman's body. An object, nothing special. *You're being unfair*, your mother rebukes you from the back of your mind. The irony of this thought coming to you in her voice makes you blink.

'What did you do? Before you...' The forensic tech gestures at you, at this scene. She means before you were called. She's wondering why you, out of all the people on this good Earth were called to this murder scene like a bird winging its way back to its breeding grounds.

'Oh, I'm...' You're about to say "nobody". You're nobody compared to the tech, no doubt she studied for years and has seen many crime scenes. 'I worked at a hotel chain's head office. Temporarily.'

'Husband?' She eyes you cannily, as if wondering if you can take this burden without a support mechanism.

'No,' you say and smile to show you aren't offended by the implication. 'Just me.'

'There are funds you can access,' she goes on. 'Financial support. If you've had to leave your work.'

You nod your head in thanks, but you won't apply. Let the single parents and the supermarket shelf-stackers who are called use the funds. Your savings are healthy enough.

You squat down beside the woman's body, reminding yourself she is Cara, a person. You resist the urge to switch a single strand of hair out of her eye. It's powerfully wrong, all of it. The dead woman can't feel the hair, it doesn't scratch at her, make her tear ducts activate in defence. She doesn't care how it looks, how she looks. But your fingers twitch in sympathetic response. You can't do much about the other horrific injuries to her body, but you could do something about the strand of hair.

No. Resist.

You pretend to look at your clipboard, at the notes they've prepared for you. But you are thinking about a few weeks ago when a man tried to force his way into your back garden, rattled the tricky back gate, too drunk to figure out if he just lifted it over the latch... How he didn't run off when you confronted him, how only your male neighbour's arrival scared him off.

You think about the smell of vodka on his breath, blowing through the gate. About the leer. You think about how little boys are not raised to care about being meek and quiet, and that frightening girls is fun.

'She was killed somewhere else,' the tech tells you. The amount of blood that isn't here means she was dumped. This isn't the place Cara died. 'But maybe since she called you, she can tell you where that is?'

This irritates you. *Not how it works*, you snap, but only in your head because you *were* raised to be meek and quiet.

'I think I've seen enough,' is what you say aloud, and you kick yourself for the "I think". You're supposed to know. Everyone else knows. When they speak, they tell the world how confident they are, and people listen. You're supposed to be sure for her, the body of Cara Ellesmere, left here as if a litterbug just crushed her up like a paper bag and tossed her out the window of a speeding truck.

You're supposed to know and force reality to fit around your knowledge. That's how the rest of the world does things, isn't it?

*

Womanhood felt like a trick when they first put it on you.

You started out playing and running around, happy, fierce, free. Then they separated you from that. Put you in skirts and told you to be quiet, and never to show your knickers to anybody. Then the boys would always make a point to try to see them, now they were there, just under the cloth, forbidden.

The knickers were always white, symbolising virginity. When you got your first periods, you'd spend hours secretly trying to scrub out the tell-tale faint marks on the gussets where the blood just wouldn't shift, too ashamed to just put them in the laundry hamper. You moved to dark underwear as soon as you had enough control over your life to do so.

You were told you had to keep having periods, that you had to take those seven days of placebo at the end of each pack of contraceptive pills. No one could ever explain why you couldn't just go on to your next pack. You had no intention of getting pregnant, why did you need to bleed? You just did, you were told. Your fertility was so much more important than what you wanted.

You were told if you worked hard and kept your mouth shut, you'd be treated with respect, just like any man. Then you found out the male graduate was being paid the same as you, even after your ten years of experience doing the job. So you quit. Got a temp job working for a hotel chain's office. So many more women. Maternity leave was common, and so was flexible time for picking up children from school. That didn't make much difference to you, but you liked the atmosphere it created. It was less competitive. You were happy there.

Then you were called. You had to ring the agency and tell them you couldn't come back for a while. They'd likely replaced you already. You realise all this will ruin your work record. You'll likely have to start again from scratch.

*

At home, you read up on cases like Cara's into the night. You hear a noise, so you rush to peer out the window for someone trying to get into your garden again. You shut off the lights to hide yourself – to make sure you can see outside – but that just means you're now in the dark. You can't see anything out there. He was just an alcoholic homeless man, you tell yourself. He didn't even know where he was. But somehow, you still don't feel like getting into your pyjamas and lying in bed. What if someone did break in?

How would they break in? You would hear them, wouldn't you?

What if you were asleep? What if you woke up with a dark figure above you? What if you didn't wake up until he plunged the knife into you, too late to scream or fight or call the cops?

Would you smell his vodka breath before you saw him?

There's nothing happening outside. It might have been an animal. Or the wind making the gate bang. It was nothing. But you're rattled. You hate yourself for being rattled. You think it's just another way women are pushed down in this world, being taught to fear. Not like their brothers, who are taught the opposite.

You've been called. You need to get it together. For Cara. Maybe you can't sleep. Maybe that's okay. You can stay up all night researching cases instead. They keep you awake until dawn.

*

One murder, one called. You don't know if double homicides call two. What about a spree killer? Does each victim get someone separate?

Yes, it must be that way. You're called to the body, not the killer. If you were called to the killer, you wouldn't have to read these reports and articles, police statements, and transcripts so long your eyes stopped making sense of the information. You'd go straight to the answer.

None of it has any rational meaning anymore. How can there be people who take other people apart? Turn them from a vital being with thoughts and hopes into just some bits, disarticulating the life out of their flesh? And some people who do it just for fun?

Your mind is so full, the thoughts all swirl into one another, tumbling on and over each question. You think about what 'fun' means to most people. What it means to you. You think about holidays. You wonder if you can go on holiday anymore. A single-occupant room is something that doesn't seem such luxury now. It seems cold. It seems risky.

People pair up in life, and so many people tell you it's okay you're single, that society's obsession with coupling is sexist, outdated. That you should enjoy your solo life. What they don't think about is that there's no one there to watch out for the creeping stranger while you sleep. No backup. You wonder how often people get married for the backup more than the other stuff. And stay that way, even when they are clearly wrong for each other.

You look up the stats: how many women go missing on holiday? You have an intuition that there are plenty who are attacked but don't report it. Like you. You didn't report it.

You were in a foreign land, a country with stricter Christian views about women having unmarried sex. You went alone, feeling independent. You wore swimwear, little shorts, spaghetti straps. Who could you tell about the "friendly" guy who forced himself on you when you were nearly blackout drunk because the booze was so cheap and the staff so happy to put it on your room tab?

No one gets called to those. No body, no call. Except you felt like a ghost, the day after.

You walked through a world broken into shards of colours too bright and painful, hungover and scared you were pregnant, or had HIV. And this, too, made you angry. Why should rape be any different to any other kind of injury? But it is. It was.

The stats are meaningless, you decide.

*

The sunlight coming into the apartment is stronger. You must have dozed off in the chair. You realise it's the middle of the day. You make coffee, but can feel the edge of a cold coming on. You can't get sick now. You've been called. Cara's body needs you to do something. To do what? You are so tired. You fall back to the doze.

You shiver awake when the memory of the homeless man returns. It prickles you. You spend a long time looking out the window. But from a safe angle, half-screened by the potted plant on the sill. He isn't there.

You didn't want to call the police on him either. After all, what would you tell them? Someone tried to get into your garden but didn't? And he'd clearly had his own problems, reeking of vodka and urine. But did that mean he was harmless?

You decide to drive around the area Cara was found. In daylight. To stay in the car. You leave your flat, go down to where you parked at the curb and perform your little backseat check, then up and down the street before you unlock. It's the first time you notice yourself doing it. Automatic, default, normal. You have your running shoes on. They're more comfortable to drive in, you tell yourself. You think about going back inside to change into your jeans, feeling the air under the hem of your skirt, but tell yourself this is ridiculous; you aren't even getting out of the car. You're just driving around a bit, getting a feel for the place; up there, on the mountain road.

*

A neighbour boy once tried to talk you into sex. You were maybe seven, he ten or eleven. He was too young to know what was wrong with it, and so were you. And you went along with it for a while. You even pulled your pants down like he wanted. But when something (you never saw what) touched you there, you pulled them up again. You walked away, fast as you could. He never asked again.

They called it 'playing doctors and nurses' back then. The doctors were the little boys, of course, and the nurses the little girls. And, perhaps it's you. Perhaps you are mistaken in feeling that this is just step one in a lifetime of normalising coercive behaviour and gendered roles. You're too uptight. After all, if nobody else has a problem with it, you're the one out of step with the rest of society.

Unless a lot of other people think that way, but don't say it out loud.

*

'Everyone gets one call in their lifetime', but that can't be right. Population numbers suggest that is impossible. And so, you're special.

You could've had a little old lady knocked down by a hit and run. You could've had a man beaten to death in a drugs deal gone wrong. But no. They didn't call you. You wonder if it is a like-to-like thing. If, because you can imagine Cara's fear, you are more likely to find her justice.

You've read memoirs about people called to cases. Just the famous ones. Just the ones that were solved. No one writes about the ones that fail. You wonder about people who are called and don't care enough to solve it. Or people who aren't diligent enough, lack analytical skills, what then?

You wonder what use you are. You feel like you have the intellect and attitude to be able to solve it, but you aren't sure you believe in justice. Not in the way it happens in society, now. The sweet and simple idea that if you are killed, a person will be called by the world to bring you justice just seems so unbelievably naïve.

If it really worked like that, there wouldn't be such hate, such violence still out there. Someone hated women so much they stabbed and stabbed, attempted to unwoman Cara. Her body said that so very loud, and the thrum of that action had passed down the threads of whatever it was that called you to her. So, in a way, they have done this to you, too.

*

You never told anyone about the neighbour kid's actions. But you did confront him once, when you were older, told him that you remembered it. You had some trepidation but enough liquid courage to not give a fuck about the consequences, ready for a fight. But what you did not expect was his response. He denied it. Flat out said it hadn't happened.

A stranger groped you in your bunk bed while you were on school camp, aged fourteen. You awoke to see a shadow standing over you, reaching down, touching your private parts. You sat up, and he walked out. You stayed, frozen, awake until daytime when you told the teachers. They said you had dreamed it. The other girls mocked you, said you were just making things up for attention. Until another girl was groped the very next night. Up until that point, when adults dashed out into the night with flashlights, they'd said it hadn't happened.

You told your mother about the time you were date raped in college. The young man engineered a situation so you couldn't escape having sex with him, wouldn't let you go until you did. This too was rape. Your mother said it was not. As if by saying so, she could make it so. She told you it hadn't happened.

It would be nice to think it was because she could never imagine something so horrible for you, that she loved you and could not make her mind encompass the fact. But you know it's not that. That stuff only happened to low-class people. Trashy, sad people. She was not the type of person who had a daughter who'd been raped. So, she changed reality to make it fit better.

You understand all these denials, really, you do. They're only human after all. But it would be nice not to be gaslit.

*

Cara's eye with the single strand of hair draped across comes back to you often, horribly and gut-wrenchingly often, as you drive up the lonely road where she was found. You wonder how she got up here, into the mountains. It's windy, cold. The landscape is brutally hard: scree, bogs, and washouts. Was she hitchhiking? In this day and age? Would you? What desperation would drive you to do that? And what kind of person would you look at and think you were safe to travel with?

Not a big, hulking monster of a man. An ordinary man, with size nine shoes.

The last place Cara was seen alive was a bar in the West End. She left, on her own, after saying goodbye to some friends. She turned off the busy streets, away from the security cameras. She might have been walking near one of the on-ramps to the motorway. But this was never confirmed. She had evaporated, as far as anybody knew.

You park on the side of the road, close to the crime scene. (It's been closed down, all the evidence taken away, down to the last follicle. There is no trace of Cara left there now.)

You check the doors are locked. You check the mirrors. The doors again. But you have to get out, you have to see. You grip the door handle for the longest time before you make yourself let go. The clunk of it shutting is as loud as a gunshot.

You hold your keys in your hand. Should you lock it? But you're not going that far, and what if you need to get back in quickly? You wonder if you should have left the keys in the ignition, the engine running, but by the time this thought hits, you're already scuttling down into the table drain at the side of the road. You strain your ears. Nothing coming.

At the bottom of the ditch, you sit down on the disgusting, greasy gravel. You lie back. You can feel every nub and jag of the hard ground. There is a vine creeping beside you, choked in particulates. You wonder if your clothes will be ruined. And if you care.

A car comes around the bend and screeches past yours, revving to get round in time. They don't see you, but you can tell they are aggravated by the sound of their engine. You wonder about that ability. So fine-tuned, an instinct like a prey animal. You can spot aggression, aggravation, from a great distance, through several layers of medium.

The car hadn't stopped. If it had, what could have happened? Could you have been murdered too?

You lie here and look at the sky. Cara was in a ditch like this, so close to here. You are Cara, but for better luck. You carry a little piece of her with you as you get up, dust yourself off. A soft piece like a feather, fragile in your heart, liable to blow away at any moment.

*

You go to see her mother, Rachael McGivern. She is a bundle of bones held together with doggedness and quiet rage. She does not know where Cara was. She hadn't been in touch with her for a little while. She felt bad that after her divorce, she and Cara drew further and further apart. She blames herself for her daughter's circumstances before she disappeared.

She is looking after Cara's son, a quiet little boy with big, troubled eyes who sits on the laminate floor, not playing with his toy trucks. You try not to think about trauma and abuse passed down generation after generation. You don't ask why Rachael got divorced.

You look around at her house and see a war being fought between propriety and mental health issues. Knickknacks, magazine piles, potted plants. Things that women are meant to have. A lot of clutter, but everything within easy reach is cleaned, polished, waxed despite all the weight piled onto her shoulders. Despite the fact she has health problems and needs a stick.

You hate yourself for thinking maybe it's a lucky thing Cara's kid's so quiet, for a little boy.

Rachael shows you pictures of young Cara, alive Cara, smiling Cara with no hair stuck to her eye. She asks you about where they found her daughter. You tell her the road name and the approximate distance along it. But she already knows that, was told by the police.

That isn't what she wants from you. But you cannot tell her how lonely it was. She reads it in your face anyway and you are sorry for putting that on her, too.

On the drive back to your place, you think about the patches of furniture dust that Rachael couldn't reach, and about her hair, so straggly in the back. You think about your own body and how eventually it might just be the parts that you can see or reach that get taken care of.

And only taken care of as far as society sees fit. You can starve yourself skinny and miserable, and this is fine. You can destroy your feet with ridiculous, painful shoes, but this is fine too. You can wear makeup to hide a bruise.

This is all fine.

*

Cara's body inhabits your brain at all hours. But you aren't only thinking about her, now, even as you comb the internet for clues. Suddenly you can *see* all the media directed at you. Makeup to make you flawless, creams to make you ageless, clothes to make you desirable.

You see advertisements that show women lying prone as if dead. You think about how dead women can be an aesthetic: slasher films where a woman's blood sprays everywhere in artistic fountains, adventure films where the hero hoists her limp form in his arms and cries his need for revenge to the heavens.

You think about other, supposedly romantic, films where men forcibly grab and kiss women and, in the film's logic, she surrenders and fall deeply, madly in love. She doesn't push him away. He doesn't slash her tires for rejecting him.

You think how women can be vessels for a man's passions, love or hate. They can be muses for his artistic outpourings. They can be his support frame, his carer, his facilitator. They can be ballbusters, or evil villainesses, out to destroy him or steal him away from his loving family.

You think about how rare it is for women to be portrayed as just people. You wonder how it got to this.

You heard the term 'political lesbianism'. At the time you thought it was ridiculous. You can't decide sexuality, you thought. But now you wonder if you will feel safe, ever again, with men. Who might seem like good guys. Ordinary, size-nine-wearing, harmless guys. Boys-next-door.

*

You stand at the edge of the shopping centre's multistorey carpark. You look out and down, over the guardrail. You think about your clothes, each piece designed for someone else's enjoyment. You dress practically, most of the time. But still. Shallow, useless pockets so the line of your thighs isn't ruined. Three-quarter length sleeves on your work shirt, because women's wrists don't deserve to be warm. Lace around the trim of all your underwear, whether you want it or not.

You envision yourself stripping off each piece of clothing and throwing it over the edge. Then joining them.

You could jump. Your body would probably split like a melon when you landed. But then who would look out for Cara? She called you.

Maybe all women call you.

*

'I have something to show the case officer,' you tell the detective bureau receptionist. She's a tired, hard-bitten woman. She wears lipstick and mascara. Her eyes are watering and pink, perhaps irritated by the makeup. You wonder for how many years. 'Cara Ellesmere's case?' You smile. It's okay for you to be nice to her. She probably has enough of a shitty time from the male officers, the banter that they use as a stick to trip all their female colleagues. If anything, it's probably worse in this environment than in any you've experienced.

She doesn't take you very seriously. 'Just sit down and I'm sure he'll get to you soon enough.'

You ask her if she could give him another call, and she fixes you with a stare from under her brows. 'He's a very busy man,' she says.

He keeps you waiting. You go home, eventually; decide to try again tomorrow.

*

You wonder what size of foot the man had, the one who tried to get into your garden.

Every click of the central heating or sound of a car thumping over a pothole in the street, day or night, jerks you out of restfulness.

He can't get me, you tell yourself, over and over. *He doesn't know I was called. The doors and windows are locked.*

He can't get me.

*

Cara's case officer opens the interview room for you to use. It is small, windowless, and though there are cameras on the wall, they don't have any recording indicator lights on. You don't know if that makes you feel better or worse.

You hesitate over which seat to take at the small desk. He motions you to the one in the corner. On the one hand, it feels good to have your back against the wall. On the other hand, he is between you and the door.

You tell yourself that he is just doing his job. That not all men think women deserve to be raped or killed; that's ridiculous. You can't live your life without trust.

You place your printout maps with their careful marker dots, maps of the lonely mountain road, and women's disappearances in the area. You show how bodies were discovered on the left-hand side of the roadway over several years, indicating the killer was likely headed north-west each time he dumped the bodies. Some were buried in shallow graves within fifty metres of a layby. Some, like for Cara, showed less care. The known point of origin for each of the women on their day of disappearance was from the West End. You tell him that the killer likely kept a regular route, like a lorry driver or a sales rep. That there was a chance he used the bathrooms of this service station, or this. And if they could recover video surveillance of those places, they might find enough...

The policeman stops you. 'You don't know it's a 'he'.'

You suggest this is the most likely case. You cite official statistics, the autopsy's findings. He curls his lip that you dare suggest you know anything about it. 'We'll be keeping an open mind until we find evidence otherwise.' He gets up and leaves, not taking any of your printouts with him.

The shoeprints, you belatedly recall. But he's gone.

You realise that in your enthusiasm to show your work, you hadn't factored in that you would need the other person to want to hear it.

*

You're a grown woman. You learned some martial arts. You reckon you could hit someone pretty hard if you needed to. And despite all this, you were rattled by a drunk trying to force his way into your garden. You still jump up and look out each time you hear a noise back there. It's been weeks since the incident, but you still dread what might happen, if next time he gets in. Because he's unlikely to be intimidated away, you wonder what you would have to do.

You could get security cameras as a deterrent. But they don't offer a force field. They didn't stop Cara's death. You don't know what she could have done; if she was surprised in death or saw it coming and could not stop it.

You only nap in the daytime now. Just a few hours, here and there.

*

You think you must have lost your mind when you find yourself driving the lonely road again in the dead of night, stopping at the service stations, drinking their terrible coffee. You think you might see him, identify him by the look on his face. Dead, cold eyes, that's what you imagine. The face of a killer.

But then you remember the size nine shoes. So instead, you look at smaller, less intimidating men. Ordinary men, who look like they have a family waiting for them back home. There are a lot of them. Some of them notice you looking. They flash sleazy smiles at you, but when you don't smile back, they tell you to cheer up, and when you don't, when you keep looking on stonily, they call you a sour-faced bitch. You note how quickly their attitude flips when you don't respond the way they want. Almost as if they didn't really care about your happiness in the first place.

You aren't a person; you're a decoration made for their world. Or, you're an opportunity.

You enter the bathroom with a kitchen knife held inside your pocket. The stalls are lit by the strips of dead, flat fluorescent light. Every sound echoes across the tiles.

You walk out as fast as you can, lock yourself in your car and hiss the adrenaline out. You grip the knife and stare.

*

The case officer calls to offer a tranche of security cam footage for your theory (that he makes sound stupid and childish). He makes you come into the station, forty-five minutes' car journey, to sign a piece of paper that promises you jailtime if you release any of the videos onto the internet or make unauthorised copies. Or even, it says at the bottom, disclose your possession of it to anyone outside law enforcement.

He asks for your email address so he can send you a download link.

You have an account that you use for spam mail, give him that, then realise this is a mistake as you drive home. Now you will have to check it every day until the case is over and wade through the messages about sales that you cannot miss for things that you would never need.

And now he has a method to contact you for his own purposes. You wonder if he will use it. Say he knows it's irregular, but he really likes you, wants to get to know you outside of work?

You will delete the account after you've finished with the case. You're not sure why him having it bothers you so much. After all, you had to give them your full name, date of birth, and home address when you became officially involved in the investigation. After you were called.

He could show up at your house at any time, under any pretext, or none at all. And no-one will do anything about it because he is the police.

*

You think about fleeing the country, leaving all the mess behind. You never asked for any of this; you never led anyone on. You were called, you did your duty. That's all.

Cara needs you. You can't leave.

And anyway, where could you go where this couldn't happen? Where women are just treated like people? Where, in all the world?

You are so tired.

*

You notice that the footage from the service stations is for the date of the victims' disappearances but does not include the early hours of the following morning. You email the cop back, and he makes you feel bad for asking. It is several months until you receive all the footage you need to complete this task. Meanwhile, you know Cara's mother and son are waiting for you to find answers.

You spend hours reviewing the footage, scribbling notes. You use terse descriptors for people. You see one and smudge the ink in your hurry to capture his existence:

- Black donkey jacket, 2 am, looks suss.
- Was at other services two hours after Jane Doe?

95

- How did they miss this guy??

He's small. Wide-shouldered but short. You can't tell exactly from the quality of the footage, but something about the way he holds himself, the way he looks around him before entering the restroom. The footage is grainy, terrible. Could he have misted droplets of blood on his dark jacket? Hands? Face?

You send the lead to the email address they gave you, give the timestamp, the horrible co-incidence.

*

You always thought you were lucky. You watched true crime documentaries, fascinated despite the sickening details. You watched how men killed their partners because they were jealous, because they wanted to end the relationship and take up with someone else, because they wanted insurance money.

Somehow those were worse than the mentally disturbed killers.

You always thought you were lucky (and you are) to still be alive. But you've been less lucky than you tell yourself. You haven't gotten off scot-free. You've been damaged. But society has told you this is what you should expect. You've been assaulted many times, when you think about it. But you didn't call it that. You called it something else. You minimised. You wonder how busy the police would be if every woman reported every time.

*

Cara was assumed to be a sex worker. She was a single mother. She may have had substance issues. A well-worn path to prostitution.

So what if Cara was doing sex work? Should she not deserve to live? You decide if there is a moral component to the right to survive, a lot of people are in trouble.

Your darker mind wonders about fucking the police case officer. Emotionless, just physical. You don't think you could do it.

*

You've been following the social media page her mother, Rachael, set up and you receive a notification of a new post.

You open it, expecting another heartfelt plea for anyone who has information to come forward. But it isn't that. Someone was arrested.

You sit bolt upright and click through to a national newspaper's article. There's a photo of the officer you met, arms folded, stern but confident. He's quoted as saying he noticed the pattern of several other disappearances in the area and linked them all up by going painstakingly through hours upon hours of security footage. He does not mention you.

There is no photo of the man they arrested. But the story says he drove a minivan, the type used by suburban mums. They give his age, forty-seven. That is all they say about him; his privacy as a suspect is kept, for now.

Photos of Cara's body have leaked onto the internet. It wasn't you. You have your suspicions of who might have done it.

*

You drive up to the lonely mountain road again. It doesn't feel safe, per se, knowing he's sitting in a jail cell awaiting trial somewhere. But you feel a little happier. You stop at one of the service stations to get coffee as a ritual, a closing of things.

A man smiles at you. You don't smile back, but you don't deadpan him. You just nod. He walks on by with his tray and you take out your phone to make yourself look busy. You're sure you can feel him watching you, behind your shoulder.

You're sure they arrested the right man.

*

It is two weeks after the arrest that the case officer emails you. He starts out by thanking you for your assistance. He says the trial will go forward. He says he kept your name out of it in case there was any retaliation or undue invasive press coverage. He says he decided it was best for you.

He doesn't mention any of the other women who disappeared who may have been linked to Cara.

He says he'd like to discuss the case further with you, perhaps in a less formal setting? Perhaps in a pub?

Even though you knew it was coming, it still makes your stomach lurch.

You delete your email account.

Outside, the wind bangs your gate. Yes, it's just the wind.

*

You make a social media account. No photo, not your real name. You start to share your life experiences online. You think of Cara Ellesmere. You think of the other women who were on that same lonely mountain road. You make some online friends.

Slowly, a flock of responses. Other women; from every walk of life, every stripe of sexuality or gender expression. All have experiences that chime with your own. All are outraged and want to know what will be done for the missing women. Some still choose to victim blame, say it was their lifestyle that put them in danger, but you can't feel angry about that. Not everyone loses their oppression at the same pace.

All this doesn't really make you feel better. It makes you feel worse, but with solidarity.

You realise that all women are called to each other. You tell them, with a post on your timeline, that you're there for them. Then you log off. Go outside. You've got things to organise.

ISADORA'S KITCHEN

Content warning: elder healthcare issues, xenophobic
attitudes

On her first day apprenticed to me, I gave
Isadora Jonen, the elanii, an impossible task.
I'm ashamed of it now, but at the time I didn't
think. (If I had, I'd have asked myself would I play with
one of their sort any more than poke a bear? Of course
not.) But she was only young, a new kitchen porter, so I
treated her like it.

What can I tell you, except I am a fool?

She followed me around my kitchen all day with her
big eyes, an earnest angle to her skinny little body,
pestering me with questions, questions, questions. 'Chef
Ana, why do you do this? Chef Ana why do you do that?'
So, after service, I sent her to scrub the frying pans but
gave her only a bucket of cold water.

At first, to her credit, she tried to do what I asked. But
when I checked on her half an hour later, thinking to
release her from the misery, I found her staring at the
still-greasy pans with an intensely calculating look.

'Have you finished?' I shouted. She jumped, which
was satisfying, but then she asked me a question which
chilled me to the marrow.

'Is this your only method of teaching? Making people fear you by asking for something they cannot possibly give?'

Firstly, having your tricks laid bare like that is very, very uncomfortable, believe me. Secondly, hazing the new hires is a fine and proud tradition among cooks. You've heard of it, right? And thirdly, this was *Maglan's*, the restaurant with my name above the door. I, Ana Maglan, was the empress of this domain and I demanded unquestioning obedience!

But Isadora is from an old elanii family. Besides magic and healing skills, they have a particular way to look at the world, one that skewers their subject like a brochette. And I should have known better.

'How dare you, in my own kitchen?' I blustered. 'You work until I tell you to stop!' She might have cursed me, turned me into a toad, for all I knew about elanii at that time. If she had not been Isadora, I don't know what might have happened. But she was, so she ignored me, calmly removed her apron, and left.

I thought it would be the last I heard of her, but no, not by a long shot.

Years later, she started her own bistro right here in town; *Isadora's*. She had smuggled herself into cold and rattling freight trains to Barcelona and then Paris, to find teachers who better suited her temperament, to learn what it was she wanted to learn. When she returned, it was in a comfortable second-class sleeper carriage, bent on opening her own establishment at the other end of town. She had travelled the world not just for experience but for inspiration, something I had never had time to do. (I'd always meant to. You're hard-working, you understand how it is.)

Any kind of artist must have an appreciation for the milieu in which they work. So, I went one night to see the place for myself. I suppose I wished to intimidate her a little, too, if I'm being honest. When she found out I had come, she greeted me, 'Chef Ana,' with utmost respect, and served me herself, placing the dishes for each course just so. Gone was the skinny little girl. She had grown into a powerful but steady presence in a dress of midnight blue, hair in a wrap of brocade butterflies, her apron like new snow. She smiled graciously at me, each time she collected my empty plate. The food was excellent.

By the time I left, I was fuming.

So how does one describe Isadora's output? Have you ever tried writing down the way a soaring aria tugged at your heart-space? Or could you describe the perfect sunset without it falling flat? Words feel insufficient and cliched, but we try. To me, her food was a love-song to the elements. Earthy mushrooms sprouted on your tongue. Fish recalled a day at the seaside, brine and sunshine dazzling. Fiery peppers, arid spices on melt-in-your-mouth meats. Desserts like a breeze blowing through citrus groves and spun sugar. All were honest but sophisticated courses. They had depth, breadth, height... And something else, something of its own. Her food was a new dimension.

I had to find out her secret.

It is a fool's errand to walk into an elanii's kitchen unprepared, so I undertook a programme of surveillance the likes of which our little town had never seen. I bribed delivery workers to tell me their manifests, I paid small boys to play outside her door and watch during the day, petty toughs to do the same at night. I often found an excuse to visit neighbouring shops, the haberdasher, the ironmonger, the tailor. Nothing magical seemed to be happening. Deliveries of potatoes, chanterelles, cheeses, shallots. Diners, well-wishers, food critics: all entered, ate, and exited; uplifted, smiling, almost glowing.

It was driving me crazy. She must be hiding something! I resolved that there must be a diabolical spell she was casting on my town and that I was the one to break it.

In truth, I needed something soon. My customer numbers had fallen rapidly. It seemed that not only were people flocking to *Isadora's*, they were prepared to wait rather than have an inferior experience elsewhere! It was the height of injustice, after my many years of hard work. Those few we did entertain seemed listless, unenthused by my food. Mayor Burgadey, one of my most supportive patrons, had defected! Whispers began to filter back to me that I had lost it, burnt out, that my food lacked a certain something, perhaps I had started cutting corners?

I admit this did little for my temper. My saucier even had to endure me pouring a too-cold pan of béarnaise on her head one night. The poor woman hasn't looked at me the same since, and I little blame her. Many staff left me after Isadora's triumph. I had to do something, you understand? And so, I put in motion the action that would seal my fate.

My night-time spies had all assured me that Isadora always followed the same routine: last patrons firmly but politely ejected by eleven, dishwashers, and cleaners done by eleven-thirty, and she the last one out and up the street a quarter of an hour later. In time to get to some midnight elanii ritual, I supposed. Naked dancing around the stones? Sacrificing goats to the starlight? Let us just say, years of vicious and titillating gossip about these people fed my imagination well.

I lingered in my own kitchen until it was at least an hour after midnight, then pulled on my darkest clothing to creep along the tiny goat paths behind our town. There was little light except some streetlamps, and window glows below me. The most part was in darkness, a mass of shadow nestled in a valley. While I walked, I tallied what I knew about her and the elanii in my head.

Of course, there were whispers about 'skyclad' dances, and secret marks on the women of these families. And that they could work magical vengeance on you if you wronged them. I hadn't seen any of this with my own eyes, but where there's smoke, you know? In other parts of the country, the elanii had been driven out of towns, into forests or on the road in caravans. We had not done that yet, and with Isadora's restaurant's popularity, it became less and less likely.

What else? I knew she lived with her grandmother, who was ancient and frail. But other than that? Not much. They seemed a people apart, though they lived in our community. And the stories we told ourselves to fill in the gaps of our knowledge helped keep them that way.

I thought if I could just see what happened in her kitchen, I could counter it. Expose her villainous ways to the townfolk. Then she would have to quit the trade. After all, people should know when they are victims of unnatural influences, yes? It seemed like the responsible thing to do.

I made down the hill towards my rival's restaurant, creeping past the backyards of houses and through narrow alleyways. The rear entrance to *Isadora's* was down an old dirt lane between a row of back yards.

I crept ever slower as I closed in, unsure if she had set magical traps as she left. I swung my legs carefully over her low picket fence and through her vegetable garden's twining vines and rows. Squash, marrow, carrots. No mandrake or deadly nightshade that I could see in the dark. I edged past a compost heap, not aglow with phosphorescence, but ordinary, smelly food scraps. I tried not to touch anything, just in case.

I rounded a pea trellis only to flatten myself behind it again when I saw that a light was on inside. She knew, somehow! She knew I was coming that night.

I considered fleeing. But then, I would never know what it was that made her food sing with notes so vibrant that mine was dulled by comparison. What spell she cast upon her patrons that they left with lighter steps, hearts, and purses. I must know!

So, I peered around the trellis. And I saw.

I expected to find her sculpting marzipan with a mystical wave of her hands. Or directing knives in a dance to chop onions and trim fine beans. Or at least stirring a cauldron with an eldritch glow. But it was not that.

Isadora stood in the window of her kitchen, crying. Not the sort of tears that could be boiled into a potion, either. No, these flooded across red cheeks, mixed with snot, and were dashed away by a frustrated hand.

Then she plucked at the strings of her apron and tidied things away. She was finished whatever she did and would exit soon, so I secreted myself deeper into the darkness and prayed to the Saints that she would not notice me as she exited.

As I waited, I considered the confusing circumstances. Why would a magical bistro owner cry hot, ugly tears? I formulated some hypotheses.

One: something had gone wrong in one of her spells, and a customer had turned into a toad. I dismissed this. My spies would have told me of any untoward incidents, customers entering but not leaving, that kind of thing.

Two: she had lost supply of one of her secret ingredients, one of the ones that gave her an edge. It was possible. I had not managed to discover any magical supplies coming into her pantry. But I could not disprove it, either.

Three: she had been rejected by her coven. They did not approve of her meddling in mundane business.

Before I could properly weigh these three options, the door to the kitchen opened and closed again, keys jangled and door locked. I waited and held my breath. Isadora walked past me, sniffing as one does when the crying is done. The squeak of the garden gate and her shadow down the lane and I breathed again. But if I were to find any answers, my night was not yet over.

I left enough time for her to turn onto the street, then followed. Around the corner, a bright spot bobbed down past where the streetlamps ran out. A small globe of light floating above her hand – there I had it, proof of magic I saw with my very own eyes! My friend, you cannot believe how perversely pleased I was. But still, I needed more. I needed her coven, her depraved ritual. I *wanted* to see those things. How much of what we think about elanii says something about ourselves, huh?

I followed her to the very edge of town where the trees grow tall and dark, and the idea of *wolf* suddenly presses on your brain. She paused at the unfenced garden of the last house and kissed the little globe of light. It flew up and broke into a dozen pieces which bumbled off into the night. Fireflies at her beck and call! Their dispersal gave her just enough light to walk up the path to the cottage she shared with her grandmother.

It was a tiny house on stilts, generations old, and the garden was so wild it was hard to say where it ended, and the forest started. I had a notion the cottage had once been isolated, and the town had grown towards it.

Everybody knew Isadora's grandmother back in the day. We were all terribly cruel to her when we were kids, but Nan Jonen was who you called to heal your hurts. I'd fallen out of a tree scrumping apples and broken my arm badly. When my mother asked, Nan Jonen had come to put her hands on my arm. They were dry, gentle, and hot as a warming pan. And then she'd put on a poultice and splinted it skilfully, and I got better. Hasn't troubled me in years, see? Like new.

But even still, I stood outside her house at night, spying on her grandchild.

There must be more to it all than healing arts, I thought. I had just witnessed weird influence over insects. And everyone knows the danger of going to an elanii's cottage, right? How children are snatched, how evil curses turn honest woodcutters into pigs, yes? So, I approached with my heart in my mouth. I am a woman grown, but it was dark and who knows what dangers waited inside?

I stole up to the window and listened. Perhaps the coven would reveal itself and its evil plans. Then I could tell everyone, reclaim pre-eminence as chef in the town.

'Nana!' Isadora's voice, exhausted, exasperated. The old woman said something I didn't hear well, but she sounded petulant. Had Isadora caught her doing something that even she disapproved of? How diabolical must it be?

Isadora grunted as if lifting a heavy burden. A body? Was there someone they had killed? That decided it, I must take on the danger for the good of the town, be the hero they needed. I stole closer. The window was just above my head, but if I teetered with one foot on the stoop, I could lean...

Isadora lifted Nan Jonen from the floor into a seat, then knelt at her feet with her head in her lap. 'You can't keep trying to get out of bed when I'm not here,' she said.

There was no coven, just an old woman patting a girl's hair as she cried. A deep embarrassment hit me, of course. It was time to leave. I stepped down, but the wood creaked beneath my feet.

I ran for the street and didn't stop until I was around the corner. But I did look over my shoulder a few times and saw Isadora standing in the light of the doorway, looking out. I ran faster. Fear and, yes, shame sped my heels.

There were a few days after that that I worried I might have caught a curse in the back. You know how it is when you think so strongly that you might be sick that it actually makes you sick? Let us just say it was a good thing my restaurant was not so busy anymore.

But during those days, I tried to turn over in my head what I had really seen. If there was evidence of magic, it was so well-hidden that it looked entirely normal. Perhaps the decoration inside was a little, shall we say, unorthodox? There had been strange, folded paper shapes hung on the walls, but I could not perceive if these were charms or just decoration. The room was stuffed with many intricately woven textiles, like the elanii shawls you see at the market. They all looked faded, worn, loved for lifetimes. There was a cauldron by the fireplace, I picked that out easily. But when I thought about it, it was hard to say if cauldron was just another word for cooking pot, the kind old women make soup in. There was no strong evidence of evil to bring to the rest of the village, eager as they would be to hear it, so I decided that I must check the kitchen once more.

This time I would go a little earlier, and catch the magic in action. I picked a time closer to midnight. The lights at Isadora's were off, but I wondered if she would return as she had the other night, so I leapt over the fence of the house that backed onto the opposite side of the lane, hoping there were no dogs.

I hid for what felt like hours, wondering each moment if I should just go, if she were ever coming, but then, there, a small light bobbing in front of a figure down the lane. It was her.

She dismissed the fireflies and went into the kitchen to turn on the lights. She was moving, I could see her back through the window, but from this angle there was no chance to see her hands. What was she doing, making a spell? Cutting mistletoe? I craned my neck.

Behind me, a beam of light flashed on in the house of the yard where I hid. 'Is someone there?' I dove over the fence and across into Isadora's garden, where I sought shelter behind the pea trellis. It was a stupid move, but I hoped it would be dark enough to hide me. I was wrong. Isadora stared right at me from her window, a knife poised in her hand.

I froze, of course, ice in my veins. Everybody knows an elanii's stare can do that, like a Gorgon. Not, of course, because I had been caught dressed in dark clothing in her garden in the middle of the night.

She dropped her chin and raised her eyebrows, a look that said, *truly?* Then she sighed and went to the door to unlock it. Perhaps I should have run. In that momentary release, I could have run. But instead, I found myself drifting closer.

The crack of light widened to reveal her face, silhouetted by the glow behind her.

'It's all right Mister Felisto,' she called to her neighbour, who grumbled but went back inside. 'What do you want?' She addressed this to me in that simple, straightforward way of hers. 'You like to watch people working?'

'But why?' I stuttered, waving my hand at her kitchen counters. I could see what she had been doing. A knife, a slate chopping board, a curled-up savoy cabbage leaf cut into shreds. Chiffonade. The regular, unmagical kind. But why would the best restauranteur in town need to work late into the night? Would magic not provide her with all the answers she needed? Some garbled version of these questions came from my mouth.

She looked at me with disbelief. 'You too?'

'I...'

'I don't use magic in my cooking, you fool,' she cried. 'The reason my food tastes so good is because I put my heart and soul into it until—' she slapped her palm with the back of her other hand '—I have. Nothing. Left!' And, to my horror, she burst out crying again. In this moment, I believed her. I, too, have shed many tears of anger and bitter frustration over the adversities of my career. I recognised an overworked chef when I saw one.

'But... I thought you were happy?'

'I am, but...' The floodgates opened once more. 'It's my dream. Mine. And my staff all have families and lives. And they don't always get everything how I want it, so after I see Nana to bed, I come back to prepare. And I work and work until I can't anymore. And I get up again the next day and do it all over. And I don't know how to make it better!'

The truth fell upon me then, like a cast iron skillet filled with smoking oil. I was criticised for working my staff too hard. And she was allowing herself to burn out like a falling star. I would go on a tirade if things weren't to my liking. She would secretly redo work behind her staff's backs rather than hurt them. It was so obvious.

'I will make you a deal,' I said, unsure of the path ahead but pressing on anyway. 'I will teach you how to ask if you teach me how to give. You are right, the secret to great cooking is how much of yourself you put in, but there must be a way to manage, so it is not too much.'

She straightened and looked at me gravely once more. 'No.'

I wasn't entirely shocked by this refusal; after all, I was a rival who stood in her garden spying on her in the middle of the night, and I recognised pride when I saw it. I had to respect it. I left, but before I did, I told her, 'When you change your mind, I'll be waiting.' And I left her garden, this time by the gate.

Over the next few weeks, I waited. It was quiet. I had dispersed my network of informants, having no more need, and no money to pay them in any case. *Isadora's* seemed as successful as ever. *Maglan's* was slowly imploding.

I sat upon a vegetable crate alone one night after a disappointing service, drinking a class of sherry I had not yet used up. I would have to let go of my wait staff soon and serve customers myself. And after that? I wondered if I would ever hear from Isadora, and then swore at my stupidity. I told myself that she didn't need an old has-been like me, that she would not come, and that I should give up. And so, I did.

If this were a fairy story, this would be the moment young Isadora knocked on my door and told me she had changed her mind and seen the error of her ways. But life is not so neat.

It wasn't until I was asleep in my home several weeks later that the knock came. I had been sleeping off the alcohol I had used to drown my obsolescence and the tiredness of working the wait shift as well as most of the cooking, when all manner of thunder came down upon my door.

I opened it.

'Chef Ana,' Isadora said, eyes wide. 'Please come. Nana's fallen, I can't lift her, please come.'

I was groggy but found myself jogging after her down the street. 'What about a doctor?' I puffed as I tried to keep up.

'They will not come,' she said, urging me to hurry up. 'They think we take food from their table, tell everyone we take blood sacrifice when all we do is try to help.'

And of course, when you think about it, women offering herbs to the poor for as little as a cake baked in gratitude would be a target for their hate. And the elanii stories make these lies all too easy to believe. But I was too busy to think about it. She hustled me into the small cottage at the end of the street, and I worried I had fallen into some kind of trap, but all these thoughts went out of my head when I heard the faint cries. If you have ever heard an elderly woman in distress, it is devastating, the worst thing in the world.

'In here,' Isadora called, and in a small, old-fashioned washroom, Nan Jonen lay in a groaning heap upon the cold floor. It was an awkward angle, stuck between a tub and a basin stand, no wonder she needed me. Even someone so frail is hard to lift when they are dead weight but, after much fluster, we lay Nan Jonen into her bed again.

I retreated to the living room to let Isadora fuss over her grandmother, but I did not leave. I should have run to the doctor. Made him see sense. Instead, I wafted around uselessly while the minutes ticked by.

The room was still different, foreign. The folded paper charms in intricate shapes. The furniture legs turned in a pattern unfashionable in this region. Even the smell in there was, you know, *different*, despite that they had lived in this town for a long time. Isadora would have lived here all her life, I realised, probably gone to the same school I had, though several years after me.

She entered the living room and poked at the fire. 'She'll be all right,' she said. Her hands still shook, the effects of the panic-rush wearing off. 'She has the healing in the family. I know a little, but...' She worried some moisture from her eyes with her sleeve. 'I wanted to use my own talents. With my bistro. I thought I might be able to change things. Make people feel better about us.' I did not know what to say to this.

She poured some water from a kettle into two beakers and handed one to me while she sank into an old, overstuffed armchair beside mine. I sniffed at my cup. It was floral and light. 'Just tea,' she said, smiling wryly. We sat and sipped for a moment in silence.

'Go on,' she said after a while.

I didn't know what she meant.

'Go on and tell me about how we... could help each other.' She examined her drink in front of her. 'If you still want.'

I thought for a minute, reheating the ideas that had gone cold. 'You are a talented chef. I would have to be blind not to see that. But you are also inexperienced. I am an old fossil, but when I don't let my temper get the better of me, my kitchen runs like a clock. Everyone knows their place and does their work to a standard. If it is not met, I ask them to do it again; I never come to redo their work because I don't want to hurt their feelings.' She looked a little annoyed at this, so I hurried on. 'Or worry about them turning on me, as I am not elanii, I suppose. But I also want to know how you do what you do. Your food... Isadora, it is a revelation. If we worked together, we might learn from each other. But I will be blunt. It would save me from ruin.'

'And when you have what you want from me, you'll leave me to rot, like everybody else.'

'I swear not.' I held up my hands in supplication. 'I know I may have acted like a fool before...'

She looked at me coldly. 'Yes, the spies were not a good idea.' I blanched, feeling pinned by that look. Had I already destroyed things before I started?

Nan Jonen sighed from the bedroom and it broke the moment. Isadora slumped into her chair, hand over her eyes.

'You would be my boss?' she asked in a small and tired voice.

'No! I ask you to give up your success? Is that what you think I want? I don't think I should be your boss. But... on the other hand, if I am honest, maybe I would find it difficult for you to be mine.' I smiled bitterly. 'I think that would only lead to more conflict than co-operation.' Indeed, I could not see anyone in command of me after so long. 'Instead,' I said, 'why not a partnership?'

Isadora stared into the fire. Eventually, I would come to understand some of what she was considering, the depth of elanii culture, and pride. It was a lot I asked of her.

Ah! My friend, the bell has rung, it is time for us to drink up and go home. No, don't trouble yourself, I will get the tab this time. No, no, I insist. But, you wished to know the story of how I, Ana Maglan, and she, Isadora Jonen, first became partners in cooking and, eventually, in life, so I hope you enjoyed it? This story is a happy one, and it ends with delicious food and full stomachs. But just before we go, let me place these little fancies in front of you so that you may leave completely satisfied.

Over the next few weeks, months, and years, we sorted out all the little details. We even moved into brand new premises. She showed me how to adjust my dishes for the fullest flavour, and how kindness could work wonders on our staff's morale. I helped her adjust the mise-en-place, instituted staff training, and time management for maximum efficiency. Our new space has twice the covers, but working together, we have more than doubled our income. Mayor Burgadey visits us regularly, and Isadora gets to spend more time with Nan Jonen, who is the sweetest person you ever met.

I learned a lot about the traditions of the elanii, and you know what? They are not scary people. They do have magic, they do. Isadora uses it. But not the way you think. She doesn't put bat wings or puppydog tails in her stew; those kinds of things are the stupid lies bred out of fear and years of gossip-whispers. Their arts are more subtle and profound than any of our ideas of what magic should be. Deeper. Broader. Higher. A different dimension. One that is placed within the heart by goodness.

And you can *taste* it.

I cannot explain it better than that. If you want to find out for yourself, head to our bistro. It's called *Isadorana*. She named it for both of us, to strengthen and commemorate our partnership – just another example of how wise she is. You should visit, no? There you'll see her talent, my efficiency, her generosity, my determination. And both our loves for food.

So, your only choice is this: what will you eat?

CONTEMPLATION

Content warning: suicide, execution, sexual exploitation

Above the stone city of Zenaria, clouds towered in the sky as they swept out away across the bight like dragons. The rain had gone with them, leaving the two perfectly unremarkable courtesans to lower and stow their umbrellas with the usual ceremony of flappings and tuttings as the streets bustled once more with cloth merchants and spice traders, courtiers, and priests.

'Look, my outshoes are completely ruined,' Renyie remarked with a tone that lacked any real surprise, or outrage at the fact that their fine leather was soaked and stretching. But Yolandra understood. The day was too *full* already. There was no room to breathe, even when the air was so startlingly fresh now it had been washed of the smoke from the executions. Such things would be of no concern, soon, in any case.

The puddles on the dusk-pink marble paving stones of the square mirrored the peculiarly sharp-edged light of a sun that had chased away a heavy downpour. The glare threw unsettling ghost images into the back of Yolandra's eyes, and she blinked and cast up a hand in front of her face, snagging her dangerously long sleeve with her smallest finger to help block it out. The entrance to the temple of the Seventy Divines glinted, too. The reflections from the gold filigree facade cast Renyie in a sickly colour. They shook their head and let out a snort that Yolandra took as ironic. And she understood. The contrast between the brilliance of the sunshine, the opulence of gold, and the delicate beauty of the work, against what the temple signified, it all added up to a hideous satire fit for any political poppetshow. And, then again, there was what they were about to do in return.

Renyie wore their yellow robe today, and she her red. The colours would be significant to those with any culture who studied it later, ones who knew the story of Mashil and Orene. Heroic Mashil, who gave their life. Innocent Orene, the trusted heroine who warned the king of a dire attack. But for now, the two resembled anyone of their class. Above the destitute, below the splendid. Well-enough off in any other city than Zenaria. But here, a peg below any real influence.

'Renyie,' Yolandra began, hesitantly, as they made for the temple entrance. 'I wonder how long they would keep me...' she said, and stuttered to a halt. She meant after.

'Yoya.' Their lips twitched, as they contained themself. Their skin was waxy, sickly, quite apart from the yellow of the robes and the light of the temple. Yolandra knew them well enough to see it, but hoped no other would. 'You mustn't think about it,' they finally said, and took her arm, a companionable gesture, but she could feel the tensing of their muscles, the twitch in their fingers.

They had huddled, shellshocked, in their small closet room in the hinterlands of the palace grounds, planning. Although, planning was perhaps a generous term. 'We have to do this, quickly, before I change my mind,' Renyie had said. And before Yolandra changed hers, or even thought.

They were not warriors, or even athletes. The two had spent their lives being decorative: wearing lovely robes and painting makeup over their flaws. Learning how to say happy, pithy things that made courtiers smile and nod indulgently as the droning buzz of insects floated around the nectar flowers in the palace gardens. And, of course, diligently saying prayers for their master at the Temple of the Seventy Divines. This temple, as it happened.

They both bowed under the lintel into the foyer and removed their outshoes to carry them, then continued on slippered feet across the smooth palandra-wood floors. The corridor was, in its way, even more impressive (or oppressive, depending on your perspective) than the entrance. Dark sculptures of gods, heroes, and monsters pressed in at them from all sides; some even loomed down from the ceiling so low the shortest of Zenarians would feel uncertain if their headwear would be knocked off.

The gateway at the far end opened out into a courtyard fully open to the sky, a city garden freshly washed and scattered with fallen purple petals from the sacred engienia vine that grew around the perimeter of the space. The scent! There was a reason this plant had been chosen to grow here. The perfume was transcendent, but especially now, after rain.

They stopped before the gravel path that edged the gardens and stooped to replace the outshoes over their slippers, Renyie grumbling at the difficulty of reattaching wet leather tongues to buckles. Seventy statues of sages and gods, holy beings, silently watched from the courtyard. And, over there in the centre, the seventy-first, a recent addition. One that spat in the face of the temple's very name.

A songbat chittered tunefully as it swung in its cage up in a far corner of the space. An attendant approached it with a long pole and a bag, perhaps insects for its feeding. It was the hour of such chores and housework: another attendant swept blossoms into the small trickle of water in the drain, more bustled in and out of the doors that opened into prayer halls, dormitories, kitchens, all the necessary things to support a working temple. Yolandra watched the people, her brow nearly halved in width from concern. Renyie was done fiddling with their shoes. They could move on. But she could not quite make that next footstep, the next part, where she entered the courtyard proper and did what was necessary.

'It is wet,' she said, doubtfully.

'Won't matter,' Renyie said with a grunt. 'Not with this filthy stuff.' They arched an eyebrow as they checked that no one had overheard the remark. But still, Yolandra hesitated. 'My love,' Renyie said, gently inclining their head towards her.

She had been part of them, of their world, for long enough that Yolandra heard every argument they said without any breath. *You saw what the Emperor did this morning, with help from this temple. I know you are afraid. But we will do this, anyway.*

Renyie merely waited, tranquil, while she struggled. 'How can you be so calm?' she wanted to scream, but there was no point. She schooled her face, brought her breath back to a measured rate. They had both been taught to mask their emotions so well. Even as children, everything was to be boxed inside their chests, no hint of turbulence in their expression, only serenity. Only lies.

'We go?' Renyie said and proffered the arm again.

Yolandra wondered if she loved them, now, here, at the end of it. What traitorous thoughts to be having. A person she had been raised to think on only as a sibling, no matter what debased behaviour they had to endure as they were traded like tokens around the imperial court. On the other hand, the freshness of the air, the clarity of fear, the *endingness* of it all. Perhaps this was the only time she could allow herself.

A drakefly hovered over the central pool, its reflection below captured in the porcelain blue of the now-empty sky. A storm, passed. A washing clean. Renyie had cried, after the executions, though Yolandra had only felt numbness. The emperor, sitting there as bored as if he was waiting for his luncheon. The mouth downturned in a permanent sneer. Not one flicker for the screams, the violence of the flames, the charnel house stench.

Unmoved; though those who watched were not so aloof. The fury had been incandescent, almost palpable. Yolandra felt it rush through the crowd of onlookers, forced to watch, through the both of them, even as tears had fallen down Renyie's face. Those upon the burning platforms had been branded traitors at a whim, as had their families, their children down to infants-in-arms. It would seem senseless to those outside the court, but Yolandra and Renyie knew enough, had heard enough chatter the courtiers they bedded thought them too low to hear. These people had been for political expediency. To show strength to the merchants of the sea, a small cadre of those richer than even the emperor, the only ones who could threaten him. What were a few executions compared to the emperor's position? Nothing, to him.

And then, he had withdrawn behind his citadel's impregnable walls, behind the swords of the hundreds of muted guards who would speak no evil of his Divinity Turettan, the Eternal Lord of Zenaria. A place that would keep out assassins, malcontent citizens, angry mobs, any agents of change. But courtesans, decorative baubles, would be expected to be there. Close to the Emperor. And, perhaps a courtesan who had witnessed a terrible moment would be allowed close enough to tremblingly tell her story to the Divine one himself.

It was a stupid plan, Yolandra realised, one with too many flaws. They could come up with a better one, a more certain one. She was about to tell Renyie as much, but they had already drawn the long bottle of horrible-smelling fluid from where it had been hidden inside their robe. It was too late, too late.

Renyie splashed some of the liquid at the base of the seventy-first statue. The fumes trembled the air, and Yolandra drew her sleeve up to her nose. An attendant saw and called. He trotted over to see why someone dared desecrate the statue of the Divine Emperor Turettan.

Yolandra moved to intercept.

'They've gone mad,' she said, as if panicked, and yet somehow getting in the way so the attendant fell over his own feet. 'You must stop them,' she begged as she pulled at his clothing like any hysterical, pampered brat might do in such a tussle. How unfortunate it prevented him from rising. Yolandra looked. Renyie had raised the jar and upended the rest upon their head, retching from the horridness of the liquid. They struggled with something inside their beautiful yellow robe, now soaked and mottled with the ill green stuff. So much for yellow. Yellow the colour for Mashil, the martyr who sacrificed himself for his country. More shouts went up, and attendants neared. Renyie finally pulled the thing free. It was a small clay jar.

'Stay back!' Yolandra warned the attendants. 'They've got a tinder pot!'

Renyie took the smouldering mushroom from the jar and held it up so they could see. The temple attendants staggered back, arms spread wide, fearful.

They had practiced what Renyie would say, back in their tiny closet room, in the hinterlands of the palace grounds. "Kill all tyrants', I suppose,' they had said, face wan with sickened apprehension. 'Live free as the bumblefly, kill all tyrants.' They had cackled with bad gallows humour, at the craziness of it all.

But the moment had come, and the only sound that came from their lips was a strangled squawk of fear, followed by an exhalation onto the tinder mushroom.

A bloom of flame that, for a second, seemed as if it were harmless, before the world exploded.

*

Yolandra sniffed and dried her eyes as the majordomo questioned her again. She sniffed and nodded, and murmured the responses she had practiced. Yes, she had gone to the temple for daily prayers. No, she had not known her friend would take such foul action as to harm the statue of the Divine Emperor. Yes, it was just that the traitor's memory would be shamed down to the last ancestor. No, she would never have allowed it had she known. No! She had not known they had smuggled bomb oil under their clothing!

This went on for several hours, but she was patient. And the tears were all too real. She had hidden her face away when Renyie had screamed and thrashed and run for the pond where a drakefly had so recently hovered in such peace. The attendants had dragged her from the burning building after the statue of the Emperor had exploded in burning shards that caught the engienia vine and set the entire building alight.

Only as Yolandra left did she look. Renyie had died face down in the pond, not at the feet of the statue as planned. But the result was the same. More or less.

Clamour outside the window, over the citadel walls as they fought to contain the city fire. It had spread to at least two blocks, if she understood the messages whispered to the majordomo by servants curious to look at her, the courtesan in the middle of such a fuss. The one in red. The one who looked like Orene the Innocent, later, if they thought about it. But perhaps that was thinking too much? She was a courtesan. A plaything. Surely it was coincident? But perhaps they had trusted her, a little more, because of it.

The man sighed as a more elaborately dressed servant bustled in. 'The Emperor wishes to see the witness,' he said, then gazed frankly at Yolandra.

'She is not fit for his presence.' The majordomo waved at her smudged face, dishevelled hair, and torn robe. We must get her bathed, change these clothes...'

No! That must not happen, not so close.

'The Emperor will not ask again,' the servant warned with a guarded expression. Yolandra's grip upon her chair loosened slightly.

'Very well,' the majordomo said. 'But you will wipe her face of this dirt as you go, at least?' he said, and the negotiation was over. She would go into the innermost sanctum of the citadel. A place she had rarely seen, and then only when the Emperor had grown bored of his normal servants and their attentions. When this happened, they would be stripped and prepared by the majordomo himself. But not today. Because of Renyie, their sacrifice.

She rose with dignity, and arranged her trailing sleeves properly, with the hidden blade safely inside its cuff. Everything boxed inside her chest. No hint of turbulence. Only lies.

'Let us go,' she said calmly. 'We must not keep our Emperor waiting.'

WOMEN OF SPARTA

Content warning: murder, violence, gore, gender-based
violence including rape, implied suicide, child removal/
adoption

I. Nyx

W**e came to** the men with our hidden knives.
We dressed like beasts, like birds. I wore a cloak
made from the wolf I hunted with my javelin,
so the others called me Wolf-sister. Fangs rasped my
scalp to mind me to vigilance, forelimbs knotted about
my neck, paws dangled on my chest. Others wore stag
antlers, or hair teased into the crest of a cock, with black
feather spaulders and spurs for a pendant. The horns of
a bull, the ruff of a lion. The beak and wings of a hawk,
the tail of a jackal. Multifarious were our costumes, for
Artemis the Huntress' sake. Each animal male; there was
purpose in that.

We came to their symposium, held in an empty bath,
in an empty bathhouse, in a town emptied by their
malice. We were greeted like sisters, like lovers. They
thought from our costumes we were artists, might dance
for their entertainment. For they had already taught us
they were mighty, had they not? Defeated women
should render themselves unto the victors, should they
not?

This was their mistake. They thought us women of Athens, submissive, obedient. We were women of Sparta.

Athena fluttered down in her owl-dress to watch, unblinking witness. She was more their goddess than ours, but she had sympathy with the plan and loved to see fine strategy in bloodshed.

We cajoled the men, bid them drink, and upon a secret signal, plunged our blades in deep. They did not cry out in surprise. They could not. They drowned on dry land, choking on their own lives. It was over in a matter of moments. The sunken bath pooled blood so deep it stained our toes above the sandals, dyed the hems of our cloaks. We dipped fingers to draw red stripes across our faces in victory.

Later, when we escaped into the ambrosial night, we held our own symposium high in the mountains. The secluded valleys beneath echoed back our song and Athena joined us again, perched up in the branches of our bower. Pan was notably absent, but Dionysus sulked in the corner for a time. 'You're not doing it properly!' he complained, but then fell silent and faded away in the face of our joy. We stamped our scarlet feet, whooped, leapt, sang, and kissed, while Nike clapped in time to our beats.

Eris was there, too, at our wild celebration. And she was more than happy to join in. She loved what we had done, the ripping of the fabric of order, the rage. She wished to ride the chaos like it was a stallion. She kissed each of us before dawn. 'I will see you again soon,' she promised. We wept when Eris left, as if she had been Aphrodite herself.

But Athena still would not speak to us, though we called to her up behind the fig leaves. She must know our pain – Hephaistos tried to rape her. She rejected his seed and dashed it on the ground, impregnating Gaia instead. The boy of that seed she took and raised; he founded a city named in her honour.

No-one ever asked Athena how she felt about this, about her mistake, her injury to Gaia, but she took the child, so one can only make assumptions. Perhaps she was angry we killed men from Athens. But gods are complicated.

We beseeched her to understand: the men we killed had been a plague upon our sisters for many moons. They waited until our warriors were far away, fighting another battle. They swept down upon us, taking what was not offered, thieves under Zeus' eye. And what they did not destroy of our bodies, they destroyed of our town. No lambs, no looms, no bread, no school. So, we had extracted a price for the blood spilled from our sisters' loins in rape. For the children whose heads were dashed against the ground, for corpse flies and ashes they paid.

The fire sank into embers, and the marks on our faces began to crust and flake away. Our vengeance was complete, but our story was not.

2. Eos

When dawn arrives, we feed each other figs and honey, play languid lays on our flutes and lyres. The dappled sun creeps up our oiled skin, but we have no eyes for Helios. In our minds, Eris still dances on the balls of her feet, jumping to drum her buttocks with her heels, mouth-wide smiles at our surrender to limb-loosening desire and ecstasy.

'There are more men of Athens,' Lion-sister remarks, her ruff of hair still stuck with dried blood. She sucks the seeds from a pomegranate in defiance of Hades, who stole Persephone for his consort. Even the land of death is no escape for us, no heed of our desires. So, we eat, suck seeds, love.

'We cannot kill them all. We are only seven,' says Stag-sister, her antlers discarded but still wearing a collar of sleek grey hide upon which she smears juice-sticky fingers.

'And our armies are too far away,' Cock-sister laments. Her hair fashion is wilting, a deflated crest, the glade littered with feathers plucked by her frenetic dancing. 'What can we do? Now that we have taken our vengeance?'

I say, 'They will send more men of Athens after us. They crawl over this land like fleas on a dog. We will have to leave this place.'

Jackal-sister grabs the tail that dangles from her belt and fidgets with it, nervously. 'But Wolf-sister, where will we go that they cannot find us?' She is young, has not so many years training to face iniquity.

Bull-sister cleans the crusted blood from her knife with a wide blade of grass. She is older, had taken a husband from the men of our village. Her sons would soon have shaved their heads and gone to the agoge. But not now. 'There will be a balance,' she says. 'These things? There always is.'

'We were the ones who sought to restore balance, so we are in the right,' Stag-sister argues. 'And that is philosophical law.' But philosophical law is not always the law of the land. And when the land is overrun by men who own women, trade them as cattle, what chance then?

Dogs bay in the valley below. We rush to the side of the glade, look down.

'We have to go,' Bull-sister says.

'But where?' asks Jackal-sister again, her voice rising in panic.

Hooting above our heads makes us flinch and stare. Day-owl. Athena blinks at us, then shuffles along her branch to fly out above our heads, pinions soft as Zephyr's little breeze, heading east.

'She shows our way,' says Hawk-sister, her feather cloak swirling out along the line of her arm as if she stretched up to join Athena.

'But east is Athens,' Bull-sister says. It is away from our desolated town, away from the graves of her sons.

'Who are we to question?' Cock-sister counters. 'Perhaps she will find us a safe route through.'

'There is no question,' Lion-sister tells us, her ear to the valley. 'We must leave now. Wherever we go will be safer than here.'

We pick up our bundles, kick dirt over our fire, and follow the goddess.

Yellow-white dust. The aroma of oregano rising in the heat. The bronze upturned cauldron of the sky. We circumscribe mountain peaks; we plumb ravines chorused by singing pines. We walk many leagues and see no man but hear their pursuit behind us, fearing the bite upon our heels. All the while, we follow the day-owl, hoping Athena holds our lives in her heart.

By dusk, we reach a cliff. Below is the sea, crashing, churning. We stand, unspeaking, as Athena circles on Poseidon's updrafts heady with brine.

'But we cannot fly,' Stag-sister says quietly.

'It is our punishment,' says Cock-sister. 'She has made judgement upon us for what we have done.'

'We did no less than the gods might.' Lion-sister is as fierce as her namesake. 'I say we turn and fight.'

But here is a goddess winging the air in front of us. 'Perhaps she is here as favour to Artemis,' I say, tasting the words upon my tongue, testing if I believed them. 'Or at Hera's command.' They fought side-by-side in Troia, after all.

The sound of dogs joins the shouts of men, clattering through the woods we had threaded. They will be upon us soon.

'If I call to Eris, will she not come, will she not save us?' Jackal-sister cries.

Hawk-sister's brow beneath her beaked hood is dark. 'I fear this will please her more.' By this, we know what she means. Our bodies torn to pieces in a frenzy. Or plunging into the sea to be lost in a tumble of salt and foam. But either way, there is no going home for us. This cliff is the end of the world.

'Athena will ask Poseidon to turn us into dolphins.' Bull-sister's words are not of a woman convinced. But as Nyx claims the world with a new night – a revolution of the heavens, a renewal of time – the waves below change. They swell luminous, fringed by light none of us have ever seen. They beckon.

The figure of a woman appears further along the cliffs' edge, just at the reach of our perception. She wears a huntress' skirt and tunic and carries a bow. Artemis. She nods to us, then points to the bright ocean and fades into the night as the din of the men crashing through a darkened forest punches our ears.

One by one, we discard our costumes. The scars have hardly healed. We look at each other in the dimness, naked in more than just our bodies. And, as if at another unspoken signal, join hands. The first man of Athens breaks the treeline.

We run for the edge.

FRUITING BODIES

Content warning: body horror, depression, divorce, child
abandonment, unemployment

I **wake from** fractured sleep and there are
mushrooms growing from my left arm. They're
popping up from that zone that wanted to be
triceps when I was younger but has now sunk into a
middle-aged woman's flightless wing.

It's a perplexing situation. They weren't there last
night. My skin had been itchy, but not erupting with
craters containing umbrellas in various stages of
unfurling. I wonder if it is to do with my emotional state.
I've been going through a lot. But those worries are a
background rumbling as I paw my skin, track the extent
of the growth.

The newest shrooms look like a verruca wart with a
deathly black spot in the centre. The next stage up, and
the mound is breached by a soft, wobbly thing the size,
colour, and shape of the stalk of a clove. Then a small,
purplish peg like a sports boot's cleat, and the mound
becomes a caldera as its edges recede. This is to prepare
for the finale – a puce toadstool on a delicate stem,
trembling with my movement.

Now is not a good time for them to come. I'm on my own. I've no-one to ask, 'Should I worry about this? What should I do?'

I pushed everyone away. I had to leave. My job, my family. I don't know why; I just had to. They were suffocating me. It's selfish, I know. A woman who leaves her children is the worst person in the world. But I couldn't live, there was no air, no space in my life. So, I left them all to be here in this small apartment with its small, singleton's kitchen and one boxy bedroom.

God. The shame. I can't stand people looking at me, even if I don't know them from Adam. I always think they look like they know who I am, what I've done. So, I shun the outside, in a fishtank made of drywall that sweats problem damp into darker corners. Am I black mould and neglect? Am I rot? Decay? Moral or otherwise? I keep looking, wondering.

The line of growth on my arm resembles a map of a forest. I used to love forests. I would go into them to walk, to hear the breeze swaying the branches, to feel the cool shade-dapples, to breathe in nature's peace. I'd do it again, if only I could transport there. If only I could walk outside without seeing another human being or their judgemental gaze. But I can't. I stay in bed. Perhaps this isn't such a bad thing.

There are fine, clean gills on the undersides of the small canopy of caps, and I wonder if they are edible, even as I feel them eating me. The fruiting bodies break off between my fingers' pinch with a soft click of detachment inside the dermal layers. The sockets they leave behind are smooth-floored, red voids within my arm. They've taken my body's minerals and fluids and used them to grow. I'm removing part of myself each time I break one off, but I can't help it. I'm transfixed.

Thoughts of going to the doctor, seeking some kind of help, come from that more sensible part of my brain. It thunders to be let in, to take control, but all that would mean putting clothing on, crushing the little fungi. Effort. I suppose I could make a shroud from a bedsheet, but it's too much to drag myself from my contemplation of my new status as garden. I'm a rotting, decorative log. Perhaps I will grow moss next.

I've been exhausted lately. Actually, for years. I used to have so much energy, life, drive. But now, I can barely make myself get out of bed, get dressed, eat properly. It's all so difficult.

Seeing my body literally burst with life and growth, though. There is fear in seeing this change, but also amazement. I'm giving birth again.

Is this love?

Calls flash up on my phone, but I don't have time for them, I might miss something. I can see an entire life cycle. A blemish to a fully grown fungus to macabre harvest in the blink of an eye. Or perhaps I've stopped blinking? Should I do something to break the spell? The question seems important, but it, too, shall pass. The only choice I make is not to choose.

Eventually, the phone's battery dies.

The nursery of my skin is the centre of my universe and I disgust and yet entrance myself as I pick the mushrooms while they grow, spreading across my skin, a front like an invasion. They leave behind their bomb craters. Or, more generously, the cherry blossom forecast in springtime Japan. Either way, soon I won't have much of me left. So, I push the mushrooms into my mouth and chew their leathery texture until I can swallow, to keep the cycle going for as long as I can. They taste metallic and alien. Yet so familiar.

The soles of my feet begin to sprout. As do the corners of my eyes. My drive to eat myself becomes futile as my lips blister and swell. And even as I hear a faraway knocking on the door, my voice is taken. The little parasols fill up my throat, so I cannot cry out for help, even if I want to.

But I do not want to shout. Or move. Stillness is best. In it, I can hear the mycelia grow, making me part of something bigger, a community with one mind. They want me and I want them. I can feel them hollowing out my body cavity with their filament roots. But eventually, the roots will reach such mass and density, they will fill me up completely.

And then, we will be one.

WRESTLING

The **Second Eye** hung two handspans above the horizon and Ellie was just about fed up with it. A wrestling contest was hot enough, but now that canker in the sky was throwing blue dots into her vision and giving her that weird, glassy feeling that preceded one of her bad heads. She would have to spin Tara to face it instead, when she could.

They'd reached stalemate, that point in the match where neither could find a gap in the other's defences, and it was the time you thought about giving up. If you wanted to win, you had to dig deep, use all the tricks and head-games you'd ever been shown. Ellie held the clinch and danced, pushed and pulled, looked for an opening while the Sticklers refereed, watching like hunting kestrels for rule infringements, judging the win.

But that was the question: did she really have it in her to win? When you had an opponent who was good, you had to want it, diamond-hard and bright, without anything getting in your head, getting in the way.

Sportswomen, their families, and wrestling enthusiasts formed the match ring. The more people watched, the bigger the ring. This one was a decent size.

People knew it would be a good final. Fellow competitors were easy to spot in their roomy knee breeches and canvas shin guards tied on with bits of string, and grass stains everywhere. But lots of folk in the village liked to guess who would win the competition and who would get the pig.

As Ellie turned, the circle of bodies whirled like that zoetrope of the woman doing tumbling tricks. The gadget was popular at the gala, people queuing up to get a peek at the little whirling drum. Ah, and it was all right for them. Down there they were betting on duck races and eating sweetjibs, but up on the moors there was none of that frippery. No bunting, no sideshows. Just the honest combat of two ordinary women, just the smell of hay and rough heath and salt sweat under the Sun and the Second Eye.

Ellie's cheek squished up against her opponent's shoulder, and the heavy-duty twill of the woman's shirt rasped her damp skin. Was Tara heavier this year? Were her muscles in better condition? Ellie had always beaten her before, but this was the prize match, and her own daughters, Mel and Ponty, were watching. After the argument she'd had with Mel this morning, she had this jangly nag at the back of her mind. And without the prize, they'd struggle this winter.

A spasm threatened. *Not now, not now.* Her old wrestler's back had a habit of laying her out during work, leaving her in the middle of the fields with no-one about to help her but a plough ox and a prayer. All she could do till it passed was watch clouds scudding over the blue, hiding and revealing that evil, bastard blot on the sky that had first come alive when she was just a bairn.

Perhaps the Eye would spit its final fire during the match. Perhaps Ellie would fuse to Tara in a lumpen mass of charcoaled flesh, together forever in this clinch.

What a thought! She wondered if she even liked Tara enough to invite her to tea, let alone that. If there were warning, she'd have to run, grab Mel and Ponty. That would be all right, as an ending. At least she could hold her girls, give them their last love.

But she and Tara were the ones in an embrace right now. They'd bowed their heads together at the start, clasping hands behind each other's necks. Respectful, almost romantic. Like the times the men came over from their side of the village hall to mix and dance, bow and flirt. But now Ellie was shoving her with her whole body as hard as she did against her plough ox when it was bogged.

'Come on, Tara,' her opponent's mam called. The shout led to a smattering of other calls. Some for Ellie, some for Tara, or just generally approving the idea of the wrestlers getting on with it. It felt like hours they'd been stuck here in deadlock, just pushing each other, testing weight with little feints and shoves barefoot on slippy grass, sweat threatening to blind.

She changed the angle of her grip and thrust with her head. It should make her opponent bend back, vulnerable. But Tara wasn't green. She twisted sharply round, swinging Ellie and forcing her to leap or lose her footing. She swore, unable to hold it in, even in front of her girls. She pulled Tara in and got back to the clinch, head up tight by the other woman's chin. It wasn't a satisfying move, but it was safe.

The match ring blurred. Ellie could barely make out any faces with her cheek couched in the hollow of Tara's shoulder. Mel and Ponty she could, though, one tucked under each arm of their grandmam. Ellie could find her girls in any throng.

This morning she'd wanted them to go over the Canticles, and that had led to the fight. Everybody knew 'learn a little before going out to sport'. And it helped to sing the words before a match. It was soothing. If they'd had time, she'd have taken them to sing it at the stones. The amphitheatre of a valley around the standing circle echoed the chants out across nature, multiplying their effects. But even their one-room house on the fringes of the village became a resonator as the words bounced off the stones of the walls. So, she'd told them to open the book.

'What's the point?' Mel had asked, puncturing the calm. 'We're all going to die soon anyway.'

'You don't know that,' Ellie had snapped, and it'd bowled on from there. In frustration, after back and forth and to and fro, she'd put a ruler across her eldest's knuckles.

Mel was reaching that time of defiance, of everything being an injustice, and this had been too much. She'd run out of the cottage, wailing words that seared right down to the bone. Ellie had wished she could take it back as soon as the door went bang. All girls went through this type of thing. But it would be much harder for her daughters. Mel was taking it bad. Enough knowledge to know what they all faced, and none of the stoicism age brought to fall back on. She'd come back soon after, apologetic, tear-faced, and they'd hugged it out.

'Shore up, dress up,' one of the Sticklers called, warning Ellie and Tara from careening into the watching crowd. Tara took her chance and burrowed her hard fingertips into Ellie's neck, making her growl with pain until she shrugged it off, nearly elbowing a bystander. That put a surge of gleeful fight back into in Ellie. There was nothing like that good kind of hurt, the kind that gave you a kick up the fundament, sang through your veins that here, now, you were living.

But she caught sight of Ponty squinting up at the sky, quickly, surreptitiously, as if she were doing something forbidden, and her heart plummeted.

The Society of Scholars had printed out pamphlets at the start of the year to be read in each local centre. These announced what they'd learned of the gas giant Lernetes – what most people called the Second Eye. The society had been studying it for decades, had checked and rechecked their calculations, but it was certain. The thing could ignite at any moment, turning their local bit of space into a 'twofold solar system'. And their world into a ball of ash.

All the science talk was a bit hard to fathom, but the gist of it, Ellie was sure, was that two suns wouldn't fit into one sky. 'Could be a hundred year from now,' she'd told Mel, and meek little Ponty, right there in the village square. After the reading, she'd hunkered quickly down in front of them, holding them by their shoulders and looking straight in their tearful eyes while people sobbed and shouted all around.

'Are you going to hold your breath that long?' She shook them, gently. 'For something that might not happen while you're living? We just have to get on with it.'

What else could she tell them? What else could she think?

There was no way to escape it. Nowhere to go either. The Society had calculated that the nearest other haven in space was further away than a hundred years travelling fast as starlight. And, even if they could make a steam engine go that fast, there was no guarantee that it would have air, water, plants, soil for tilling. So that was that. Everyone was stuck here, waiting for the blow.

They said Annie Longstone over at Foxhead was a natural leader, a temple deacon with fire in her veins. And she'd led her followers right down a coal mine, claiming it as a place to wait out the apocalypse, but the miners had just grinned and turned off the pit pumps.

There was a party of weavers further down the valley, too, who'd smashed up the steam looms at the mills, saying it wasn't worth working when the world was going to end, but they'd crept back, meeker, and for much less pay, when nothing had happened for weeks on end, and their stomachs had grown empty.

People blamed science, women's pride, men's wantonness, the Church of the Stones, the Church of the Air, and all these new churches popping up like mushrooms on a cowpat. Blamed everything but chance. Ellie had nearly been swept up herself when pamphleteers threatened to blackball her from the wrestling if she didn't join their march down to the Society to demand they fix things.

Ellie had asked her how they were supposed to fix anything, and the woman had got mad, red-faced, threatening that tosh. But then Ponty had come to hook herself under Ellie's arm, and the pamphleteer had gone off sour-faced. Turned out they didn't find enough folk to do any demanding. They'd had to cancel the march.

A leg stole round behind hers, going for the flip, and it was only grace that allowed her to step aside from it and force Tara to backpedal. Aborted cheers came from the circle. It was a beginner's mistake to let her get that close, sign Ellie wasn't in it, wasn't here. She needed to think strategy.

They were both strong. Tara was a dairy worker, used to lifting churns and babby calves for a living, and Ellie had to shift stubborn oxen and even stubborner stones around the fields. It was a near-even match. She still had to answer that question. Did she really want to win?

And the point of wanting anything if the whole world soon be blown to flinders?

Her mam had been a wrestler, her mam before her, all the way back to the warriors of old. But back then, they had no thought about cankers in the sky, twofold solar systems, imminent annihilation. Just who to fight next.

Would she even have had her kidlings if she'd known what was coming? If she'd known what the horrible smudge in the sky meant?

'Ellie, get your mind in the game, girl,' Mam shouted. Her mother's shadows, twinned by two lights in the sky, stretched out long across the match ring, with littler adjunct shades beside her from the huddle of her granddaughters. Foothills to her mountain.

Mam was a strict coach, using every Godsday to train Ellie since she was a toddler. Started her simple, with the dance of weight against weight. A basic leg-sweep. Shinning didn't come till later, but Ellie's lower legs had been a mottle of blue and yellow-green spots for most of her adolescence. Kidlings were allowed to stuff straw in their socks for matches, but Ellie's mam had told her, 'No point in training you up soft.'

She tried one now, a swift shift of balance, a shinbone the hardness and density of an iron bar arcing towards Tara's. Not towards the knee – that was illegal – but close. The trick was to catch the right angle, so it hurt them and not you. But Tara saw it coming and thrust her hips and legs back to the limit of how far she could go without losing the clinch. Ellie pounced and pushed down, trying to make Tara go flat on her face. But Tara dropped her weight and resolidified her stance.

The circle of watchers cried out in exasperation. The chance was gone. They muttered their disappointment, then back to tense silence, critical gazes on each foot placement, posture, movement of the women in the ring.

Back to stalemate. But Tara was getting tired, Ellie could tell. Something about her movement that she could sense without even looking. Knew it like she knew breathing.

She'd tried to teach her girls wrestling, but teaching was a different skill to doing. She wasn't able to translate things she knew so instinctively, so she'd asked her Mam to do it. It was no bad thing, recognising you can't be best at everything. And Mam had been patient with Mel and Ponty. Soft, even, which was a point of bitterness on Ellie's part. But then, even Mam was affected by the threat of the Second Eye's opening. What was the point of pushing the bairns too hard?

'What's the point of wrestling?' Mel had complained just before the ruler had come smacking down. It was what had really sparked Ellie up this morning. 'What's the point of anything, now?'

'To be better than you were before!' she'd thundered back.

It was a trite answer, but it was true, despite it all. She saw it at the standing stones, the loop of blue sky above, the thrust of the green moors, and that moment of recognising your place as a speck of next to nothing in it. All you could do was measure yourself against your best.

And now she was here, finally, in the circle, on the moors, in the match. Her head was finally here to win. But her back twinged, and the pain loosend her fingers for an instant. Suddenly, the earth was rushing up to meet her. Tara had hooked her ankle so quick she hadn't had time to adjust.

Ellie hit the ground, hard. Nobody could break the fall of something that quick, no matter how much practice they had. She gazed into Tara's shocked face. The woman was still gripping her, crouched in that last contact of the dance. The Sticklers' shout of 'match' broke the moment. Her vanquisher let go, stood up to bound around the field, throwing up her arms to celebrate her victory. Just as Ellie might have done if the positions were reversed. Tara had won the prize pig.

And now all that was above Ellie was the sky. She rested on the ground to catch her wind, looking up at the Second Eye. It seethed and roiled up there, over her daughters, her mam, the mills, the moors, everyone.

Laughter crept in and filled her up. Soon she was hugging herself on the grass. Mel and Ponty ran over and peered down at her. 'Why are you laughing?' Mel asked suspiciously. She paid no attention to what her mother was looking at; losing wasn't a laughing matter to a girl of her age. And Ellie was glad. Glad neither of them followed her gaze.

Her sides heaved, and she puffed and sighed and wiped tears until she could answer. 'Because,' she told her two girls, looking at both of their beautiful faces, 'there's no shame in losing to a stronger opponent.' They didn't need to know she meant it for more than the match.

The ring of observers dissolved into individuals again, and the people drifted off, Tara in a knot of admirers. Ellie got her girls to pull her up to her feet again, and they groaned in mock dismay at how heavy she was. Soon, even Mel was smiling.

And they'd go down from the moors to the gala to watch the bonfire and eat crackling and blueberries wrapped in summer salad leaves. And the men would dance, and the women would drink cider all night. And Ellie would sit on a bale of hay holding Mel and Ponty tight and kiss the tops of their heads till they drowsed off to the good scents of woodsmoke and apples and the hum of people all around.

And they'd deal with tomorrow tomorrow.

THE POWER OF NEGATIVITY

Content warning: racist, sexist, homophobic attitudes

When I got on the bus, I was feeling relatively happy, but that would never do. I was the only passenger and laid down the money for my fare sourly on the grimy little tray. The ticket was overpriced, and yet, I'd still be doing most of the work. But I had to pay through the nose to cover wear and tear and stockholder's shares. And the disgruntlement of the expense all helped the overall performance of the vehicle. The company would often point this out in an anonymous response, buried deep on their website, to any complaints. I took my ticket and sat down.

I straightened my rough tweed skirt as much as I could and pawed through my oversized and impossible-to-find-things bag where I'd set it on the seat beside me. The bus driver had got herself here with early morning lamentations about having such a horrible job, no doubt, but I caught her face tilted up to the circular mirror near the driver's seat, looking at me. I was extra weight. I'd need to chip in. The embarrassment of not being able to find what I needed was helpful – the electric fan on the back of the bus spun up.

I finally located my phone and started scrolling through social media, and the bus engine pootled into life. I sent a few messages to my friends, complaining about having to go to a job I detested. Hopefully, that would help them out on their morning commutes, too. No, mustn't think about helping. Not friends, either. Just people I know. People who wouldn't check I was all right if I dropped off the face of the Earth. People who only ever cared about themselves, as I did, as was the way of the world.

I posted some outraged opinions on a news comment section, and we really started to pick up speed, but it was hard work, being the only passenger. So when, at the next stop, a pair of women came on already having a loud and obnoxious conversation about a scandalous celebrity who thought herself better than other people, I felt a momentary relief. But of course, I had to go back to it.

Stop after stop, more people got on, many commenting on the driver's gender, which helped us pick up. Then there were the social media scrollers like me, aggressively misanthropic; armchair sports referees; state of the economy denouncers; death metal listeners with leaky headphones; manspreaders; mothers with babies they refused to comfort; even some school children laughing nastily at a loudly played video – we all paid our dues.

But it was exhausting. At one point, I put my phone away and looked out the window. This sparked a cascade of passive-aggressive looks and whispered comments, though, so I was still doing my bit even while doing nothing. Besides, my skirt was itching my legs intolerably, which would keep a good background level of irritation going.

I let my brain go fuzzy as the gardens and houses of the town whizzed past. Not as fast as I'd ever seen. The days after the big matches were some of the best for speed. Football hooligans had been known to light up an entire city for days. They were quite the asset to society.

The bus wound out of the suburbs and into the countryside, noticeably slowing as the green hands of nature reached out to stroke minds. The engine struggled through a dip and up the opposite slope. 'Ought to build houses here,' one man ingeniously said so the whole group could hear him. 'Rich farmers hoarding land, so we all have to live in tiny flats.' This helped the bus get over the first hill.

I continued looking out, remembering my childhood. For a few moments, I was back, playing with sticks, paddling in the river, building forts. I felt the bus shudder, but it didn't slow much. My regret that I was no longer a child meant there was no overall change in velocity.

Younger children were not expected to contribute to the energy needs of this world. They were allowed to be happy. Even if we sometimes fought, or aped our parents' cold and tempestuous behaviour, there was no overall benefit to doing so, and the next day we could be happy again.

As a grown woman, I contribute quite a lot of energy to the system. Men treat me as inferior, an object of scorn and patronisation and sexual harassment, so I feel a lot of resentment. I can keep my entire office lit up like a Christmas tree just by sitting at my desk quietly fuming. A lot of companies hire women to keep the place running. And then pay them less than their male colleagues. It's a neat little loop of fury.

A strange thought sprang into my head as hawthorn hedges and sheep passed me by. What if the technology, or engineering or whatever it is, that allows us to power our lives this way could have its polarisation switched? What if we could run everything on positivity?

I shook my head. *Stupid girl.* I was always safe thinking that. It was what my parents taught me, it's what I used to keep the lights on at home when I was otherwise content. And anyway, it would never work. What was there to be positive about?

At a stop on the fringes of the next town, a man boarded who looked like his family might be from India, or at least South Asia. His clothes were neatly pressed and clean, but not particularly fashionable. His complexion was deepest brown and his demeanour shy.

As soon as the other passengers noticed him, the bus engine revved and raced. People of a different ethnicity or religion were a favourite target of abuse, even more so than women or homosexuals. Someone shouted, 'Go back to where you came from!' and the bus driver had to apply her brake before we shot off a curve in the road.

The Asian man stood with his head down, hanging onto the upright pole near the front, jounced about by the driver's aggressive manoeuvres. I turned back to the window, but there was nothing to look at except dingy flats above shoddy shops. I checked my phone apps again, but I'd read everything shocking and outrageous already. Finally, I glanced back up at him, under my lashes, trying not to be caught staring.

There was a seat next to me that I'd selfishly blocked with my belongings. I weighed up what would happen if I offered it to him. A brown man sitting next to a white woman? I guessed I'd still get to work on time, perhaps even early. And perhaps, for once, I could do something other than quietly fuming for a while, something bold. Something rebellious.

I took my bag off the seat and met his eye.

WIGHT-SONG

Content warning: slavery, bleeding

*S**ing with me,** wind in the trees, water caressing the stones.*

If I close my eyes, close them tight enough to let my mind go back, the sounds of the spaceship's cafeteria fade. No cutlery rattle, no crew chatter. And the cave – my cave – can be overlaid. My misty mountain, my ever-home, a handful of light-years from me now. Memory calls it to me across the vastness of the void.

And it is a truth that memories have a magic all their own, that cannot be stripped by enslavement. Or science. My body is on this ship, but I live in my cave. I listen for the drip of condensation from the rocky ceiling. I hear the song of the spring that threads between the stones of the floor. The slip of pebbles, the furring moss under my hands again. Arachnid and insect feet ticker on my skin, reptile scales wind and slide along the bumps of my spine.

'Asset 3.' A voice. Far enough away I can ignore it.

Hag, wight, ice witch: what I was known as then. I call myself a different name, one unpronounceable by mortal tongue. I can almost hear it even here. I walk the ship corridors, and sometimes the humans play sounds to soothe their homesickness – wind through pine needles, the cries of birds – and I catch an echo of my name. It is filled with all the longing and promise of sunset angling into my cave, burnishing slate and granite into a glowing fall of rose-pink and grey. My true name is a meditation and a spell.

The crew call me something different.

'Asset 3!' The voice finally breaks through. I open my eyes and look at the table, at the plate of what they laughably call food on this cleaver-of-the-night, this sky fucker. I keep my head down, don't respond to the one who calls me.

'Asset 3, I got a job for you.' The meal is a puddle of congealed sauce containing stiff chunks of processed fungal protein product. 'Come on, I don't have time for this. Now.' The tip of a shock baton lands on the table, making the plate jump. I rise. Obey. I note only that my summoner wears the orange jacket of the cryonics team. I am their slave, I don't owe their personal details my attention.

They lead me down the dark blue line on the floor until we arrive at the sleeper storage bay. It is the one part of the ship where they want me. In the cafeteria I am tolerated if I sit apart and quiet. In my antiseptic quarters, devoid of soft moss or spider friends, I am deposited. What's best is if they don't have to look at me, my white eyes, my hair that falls around my shoulders in damp ropes, my emaciated frame, my hanging breasts covered by a white paper suit. I am a bleak reminder of the natural world they left behind, its darker places. And what they did to it. But here, among the stacked ranks of sleeper pods, I have a function. I am needed. I can help them "Escape to Cygnus 4!"

The orange jacket meets another. I designate them Left and Right, for they are not whole people, not even as real as the persecutors of a thousand years ago, (witch-finders, questers, misled fools). In comparison, these two are just specks, part of the ship-machine that grinds up space and time for profit.

'Well, I brought her,' Left hisses, 'but she freaks me out.'

Hollow laughter from Right. 'You don't have to whisper. It don't matter. She's dumber than a dog. Just put the thing on her. Careful, dogs've been known to bite.' Right is filled with wicked malice and lies. I don't respond because they stole my life, didn't earn my conversation. And I don't, have never, bitten.

They wrestle a harness with wires and rings and a baleful, metal eye over my head and fasten it so the iris sits on my chest.

'Asset 3,' Right says loudly and slowly, as if I am frail of mind, 'we're going to move you over to activate this casket.' I have done enough voyages now to understand that this is unusual. To wake from cold death is unpleasant, reserved for the end of a voyage. Or to wake a whole rota of crew, not just one. The sleeper must be important.

They position me in front of the pod. It is a thing like a large insect egg, white and smooth. A blue eye shines from its surface, the twin of the one on my chest.

'Okay, ready?' Right says to Left.

'Ready. Three, two, one...'

The blow always seems unnecessarily hard. I think it is a function of their fear. They could press the activation pads lightly, but they don't. They thump my back and scuttle away like beetles from a lifted rock. The mechanism starts its work, and the familiar sickness comes on as the science that dams my ability changes, opens it up.

My guts swirl, my muscles tense, my jaw gapes in a rictus, feels as if it will break. Then the atrocity of forcing open my magic. It is as if I am being torn into two thousand pieces or falling into one of the black holes this ship takes such care to skirt. My magic pours from me into the thing on my chest. Tendrils, claws, tentacles, hangman's ropes of magic build, scrabble inside the eye. A keening. Is it me? Is it the mechanism?

Then the dam bursts.

Green-edged black lightning bolts across to the corresponding eye on the sleeper pod.

It is done.

I rock back and forth, shudder, sway, and collapse. This happens each time, but they never put padding beneath me. That would show they cared. Neither is the cold hit of the floor relieved by the mineral map of veins and strata and infinitesimal detail like the stones of my cave. But I close my eyes and overlay the images of love and home anyway. It is my only haven.

Left and Right make commentary above my head.

That was unreal / she's such a spooky bitch! / is it working? / indicator's green, should be any moment / there it is, cryonic pod 859 open / welcome back Minister!

*

Nobody appreciated my ability in the old days, my misty mountain days. When beasts came to pounce and bite, or people came to rob and kill, I could stop them in their path. So, stilled, they could learn their errors slowly, in a state of grace, never ageing, never succumbing to disease. My silent friends.

But this earned me no praise from the quick. Nobody knew it was, in fact, a gift, until humans turned their faces to the stars. Suddenly, my evil became a miracle. A way to cross vast distances. A way to trick time. So, men with science came to break me, enslave me.

Temporarily, they have succeeded. But I want to go home. And I have a plan.

*

Sounds of pain and shivering. A cold-rimed voice like the grinding of a glacier, yet without the grandeur. 'Are we there?'

Left and Right don't know what to say to this personage of importance. 'Uhh, we woke you a little early with the permission of the Captain, Minister,' Right begins.

'How early?'

'Hundred-forty-nine years out. Sorry, sorry, I—'

'So, you let this thing,' a sneer, hate-filled, 'do its unnaturals on me? When we haven't even reached the colony?' There is a pause filled with menace. Then a bout of coughing. Finally, 'This better be good.'

Creaking plastic, grunts of effort, the Minister sits upright in the casket. Rough hands pull me up and out of the way. I should not impede the descent of angels to this flat white plane. Shoved in a corner, I am a thing used, forgotten.

'There is an emergency,' Left says. 'We had to wake you so the Captain and you can do a consult. Uh, I'm not supposed to tell you more until—'

'You dumb fuck,' the Minister spits. It seems this ship contains people who only kick those below them. Their treatment of me was a clue, in retrospect. 'Tell me what this is about, or I'll have you cleaning toilets by the end of shift.'

My nose has started bleeding. Red drops on the floor make tiny crowns and satellite splatters. I feel beads of liquid running down my face. I could wipe it off, but what would be the point? I am sure I look nightmarish. But I have suffered far worse.

*

When the colonists boarded the ship, they took three enslaved beings, three assets. One was originally from the Carpathians. One was a newcomer to Olympus Mons on Mars, following the human diaspora. And me, from my misty mountain that never had a name except 'home'. Our task was to put all the passengers into their frozen, dormant state. What was once our protection, the freezing of a threat into a state of grace, became a utility. We froze and thawed, froze and thawed. The magic was reaped from us again and again.

The other two were kept behind on new colonies that feed these people and their desperate expansion, their devouring of the galaxy, but I was sent on again, exhausted, wrung out, pressed into waking crew in time of need.

And it is not my first time across the void. I have been on several trips. They do not allow me the grace of cold sleep, so I have lived each trip, hour by hour, torn from my home for centuries.

*

Left and Right appear flustered by responsibility. They have woken the Minister, now they must explain why.

'There's a weird error in the navigation system,' Right says. 'Got us pointed dead at a singularity.'

The Minister's lips go thin, and there is a grunt of consternation. I have to suppress my laughter.

'We got our best engineers on it, but they can't seem to change it,' says Left. 'Captain wants to know what to do.' They gesture at all the other caskets in the sleeper storage bay. 'Got a thousand paying passengers, got five escape pods. Fit maybe ten to a pod.'

'What?' the Minister says faintly. I can see the terrible calculations crawling across their face and white all the way around their eyes.

'Cost-saving measures,' Right says sadly. 'Sanctioned by the umbrella corp. All legal, they tell me.'

Energized by this news, the Minister springs into action. 'Take me to the Captain,' they order. Such command, such ownership. I know they go to save themselves. It is written into every angle of their gait, the white clench of knuckles, hunch of shoulders. They will let everyone else die. This is a ghost ship already.

They all forget me, Asset 3, in the face of their mortality. Just like I planned. One slip of magic inside their navigation computer and their actions became inevitable. They hurry from the storage bay. I slide down into the corner, curl up over my blood splashes, and pull my cave memories around me again.

Only this time, the caskets, the cryonic pods with their sleepers, are here with me too. They stack themselves impossibly inside my memory, fold into its dimensions.

I should let them die. None are blameless. They turned their eyes away from my suffering because it was not as important as their convenience. But, I think, but. They have been betrayed too.

I should let them fly into the singularity without me, and let them be crushed by their lack of magic, by their easy collaboration with my oppressors. They should be flattened into filaments thinner than gossamer and long enough to stretch from my mountains to the moon.

Please, they say, *please*.

Despite what they think, I am not a monster.

'Very well. I will take you with me,' I whisper to the huddling shapes, the cold hearts.

My misty mountain cave is deeper and more mysterious than humans could ever know. And my magic is an underground river-twist through nature itself. It will meet us at the black hole and take us where they will never find us.

Sirens. Shudder-thrum. The awake humans are fleeing this ship already, though they know they're far from help. They will die, but in smaller groups. They hope against the vastness of space.

Silly creatures.

The black hole will become a tunnel home. When I get back there, I will surround myself with my bugs and snakes and the sleepers and sing to them about my love, the love I can feel with my fingertips that trace the wetness of the stones, the draping of cobwebs and mould. They will all know peace.

Sing with me, wind in the trees, water caressing the stones.

Sing a song through time, and the universe loses its bones.

A FEAST OF DEMONS

'**We must have** the good tablecloth. And candles.'

Mam said it straightforward as she always did, expecting us to jump to, but there were a shake in her voice. Da touched her shoulder and looked at her kind, and she burst into tears. Understandable, I s'pose. It were my sixteenth birthday, and the feast of demons came tonight.

He gave her a cuddle and looked over her head at me, a softness to the craggy lines of his brow. 'We've brought two bairns through this before,' he said, as much to me as her. 'Nowt to say we can't do it again.'

Da always held he were an Epicurean, and Mam a Stoic, but somehow, they always met in the middle. Whatever that means, he always knew just what to say to set her right again. She squeezed him, once, tight, before getting back to her preparations, and I swept the flagstones some more. She'd been cooking all day while I cleaned house, and Da had bought the fresh meat and dug vegetables from the garden.

After this one scary moment, if all went well, I'd be officially grown. No more tellings-off for fighting with the boys, no more punishment lines chalk-scratched on a blackboard for having a mouth on me. I'd be free to do as I pleased. On the other hand, there were kids who didn't pass, and they were dragged off to the otherworld, slaves forever. And what I planned to do flew against all advice on how to deal with demons.

'You all right, Annie?' Mam asked, looking up from her vegetable peeler while her hands kept right on working. I were staring into space, my grip shaking on the broomstick. 'Come back into your skin,' she said and didn't look away till I started breathing again.

'That's my lass,' Da said as he stacked firewood by the hearth.

I know Mam and Da love me; never say it, don't need to. Why would they go to all this trouble if they didn't? I know I've been mardy with them a lot, recent.

'You're a growing lass, Annie,' Da told me a few months ago. 'You don't always need to do everything right away. Give yourself a chance.' That were after they caught me kissing Michael Tobermory in the alley at the side of the bakery. Weren't angry about it. But they told me off brisk anyway. Said it were for my own protection. I sulked a bit, I s'pose. I were nearly sixteen and still treated like a babe. And yet. Now it were my birthday and the feast, suddenly being a kid forever seemed like a good idea.

But I'm no coward. I might be limited by what people say girls can and can't do, but not in my mind. I'm as brave as any of the lads at school. Braver, times. I just wish I could tell Mam or Da what I had in mind, but they'd never let me do it.

'Set the table, Annie,' Mam said, and for once I weren't annoyed at the chore. Laid the cloth – best white linen, crisp under my fingers – four places to arrange. Mine, at the head of the table for the first time in my life, maybe the last. Mam to my right, Da to my left. The fourth spot were opposite me, at the far end. This one had the special setting. A soup spoon, a fish knife, fork and knife for meat, a dessert set. Three drinking vessels: a wine goblet, a tumbler for goat's milk, a shallow dish for pig's blood. Everything down this end were made of pottery or wood. Demons couldn't abide iron, it made them angry. Last thing you wanted.

We prayed that evening on our knees by the fire, although my stomach were empty and sore. No food could pass our lips from dusk until the witching hour when the visitor would come.

'It's time,' Da said. He stood up, walked towards the door, his trick knee all stiff. Mam and I withdrew to the table. She lit the candles. I shook the blood back into my legs subtle-like, hating the ant-crawl feeling, but at least it were a distraction from the cold dread.

Da opened the door and stood back. We waited.

It seemed like hours passed, but then I looked at the candle in the middle of the table and it hadn't burned down at all, and when I looked back, there were shadows at the door. My heart lurched. They were here.

'Annnnnie,' the black shapes sang, disjointed, wrong. 'Sixteen times round the sun.'

I held my breath.

'We have laid a feast, in accordance with our laws,' Da announced. 'One of your number may enter and eat.' For the first time in my life, I detected a trace of fear in my Da's voice. I looked to my Mam as the darkness gathered in the doorway, her stillness broken by small shudders of rage.

When we were wee, Da loved telling us kids about how he'd met Mam. He'd found her on the road from the village to the town, fixing a wheel that had come off her milk cart. He'd offered to help, and she'd said, famously, 'No man's going to do a better job than me!' They'd laugh as they told it, their eyes dancing. I wondered what a woman who'd fixed cartwheels and raised three children with an iron hand felt at this kind of helplessness.

The shadows slinked into the shape of a tall, thin man. And the demon stepped into our home. 'A feeeeaaaaaaast,' it said, its head going this way and that, like a cat eying a mouse. It were naked, so I kept my eyes on its head, though that were little comfort.

'Please,' Da said, offering the demon its place at our table. We all stood until it sat.

I had not been allowed to sit at feast for my brothers. It were too dangerous, my parents said. I'd heard stories, though, we all had. Us village kids loved telling tale of Tom Moorcock whose family had not salted the demon's pork enough and how it had opened its mouth boy-wide and eaten him instead. Or the time Cynthia Toombs had spilt the goat's milk from the tumbler and disappeared in a flash of fire that burned her family to ashes. They were fables, but we also knew there were truth there, too.

When I were old enough to start wondering things, I'd asked our schoolteacher if they had the demon's feast in other parts of the world. She'd looked at me with her eyelids half-mast and told me to get back to my times tables or watch out for a paddling.

So, I'd hunted answers in the only place I knew I'd get such things – the rectory. I got a job as the Rector's maid for the summer and cleaned and dusted and mopped and waxed, all for the chance to sneak into his drawing room with its shelves on shelves of books and read for a few minutes at a time. I'd found the answers all right.

Only here. Only in this county, and just in the Uplands, did we have a demons' feast. Father Erasmus Leigh had made the deal to save the villages and towns of the region from a plague that had been wiping entire families from the parish records. And this were the deal:

no one would die from the plague for a hundred year, but the demons got a chance to try and snatch a young 'un on their sixteenth birthday. Father Leigh thought he'd been all clever when he'd thrown an ending on the bargain – "But if the child be well-mannered, so shall it be excepted".

It weren't easy, reading in words so cold and proper that if I were born almost anywhere else, I wouldn't have to face this. But my eye'd caught the dates. I'd never heard this bit before. I'd shaken my head, looked again, thinking I must be mistaken. But I weren't.

The smell of the demon jerked me out of these thoughts. It were like tar, stale pipe smoke, the back end of a cow, decay in a swamp. Then I thought, no, those things aren't evil. They're just things that happen. What were coming from this shadow-man, this darkness, were not like those things. It were *gleeful* in how much it stank. I tried to ignore it.

We all took our places except Da, who brought the tureen from the range. He placed it on the trivet in the middle of the table and looked at me. I got up, picked up the ladle, and took off the lid with a cloth. Clouds of savoury steam came up.

'Soooup,' the demon said. 'What kind?'

The hairs all over my body stood up. That voice. 'Turnip, if you please,' I said. I lifted a ladleful out, noticing my hand shaking, the stem of the spoon knocking on the side of the pot. I breathed, like Mam had told me – three quick, thin breaths through my nose, followed by one long and deep. And my hand, miraculously, steadied. I spooned one, two, three measures into the bowl and placed it in front of the demon, careful not to disturb the wispy fingers of black smoke that rose from its arms.

I filled our bowls. Enough to be polite, but none of us were that hungry. The demon's smell were making even my panging stomach curdle.

I sat, and we began the meal. 'Mmm, yesss, goooood,' the demon said.

The soup went down my own throat like it were made of knives and gravel. I could see the demon opposite as it ate. Its lips were horrible, puckered, and opened wide to show a completely round mouth with rows upon circular rows of teeth. The only thing I'd seen quite like it were the inside of our pepper grinder. Or one of the Rector's books which had pictures of deep-sea fish. P'raps both. It had a livid tongue, too large, obscene. It tipped its head back and poured each spoonful in, while lolling that tongue about. We'd have to burn the tablecloth after.

When I served the trout – whole, baked with dillweed – the demon grabbed it by the tail and used those horrible teeth to crunch head and strip bones, flakes of fish meat flying everywhere. I were glad to be at the far end of the table. My parents ate in silence, doing that thing where they talk only with their eyes.

In the middle of the meat course – carved roast beef, potatoes, carrots, and peas – the demon stopped its gobbling and looked at me. I felt pinned to my seat by eyes like the shiny side of a piece of coal. 'You have been a goooood girl, yesssss?' it asked.

I weren't ready for the question.

'She's a good girl,' Da said quickly.

'Nnnnno knowledge then?'

Mam and Da looked at each other, then at me. 'You mean...' Mam asked shakily, 'you mean carnal knowledge?'

The demon said nothing but smiled, hideous and nasty.

Mam started to say, 'Of course not—' but I cut in on her words, overtaken by an anger that made the room tilt with its strength.

'And what if I did? How would you know?'

'No!' said Da and at the same time, Mam hissed at me to shush.

'I could checkkk,' it said, 'if you liiiiike?'

I'd read up on some of this, too. A different kind of knowledge. More dangerous than a bit of a fiddle with a boy round the back of the hayshed. I had read the Rector's books. And his journals too.

'If you did, then I would have carnal knowledge, wouldn't I?' I had come to my feet. 'Because you would have given it to me! You like tricking people, don't you? 'Specially girls!'

Mam were pulling at my sleeve, trying to make me sit back down and at the same time trying to placate the demon. 'She didn't mean anything by it. Wouldn't you like something for dessert? More pig's blood? More wine?' I shook her hand off and she turned her face up at me, a look so desolate it almost made me buckle.

'Now, Annnnnie,' the demon said, sounding less oily, more angry, 'maybe I will take you with me, then you will have alllll the carnal knowledge you neeed. Forrrevvvver.'

'Except I won't go,' I said, still not as confident as I wanted to sound. 'You can't take me.'

'Why are you doing this?' Mam said, her voice so high, like steam escaping a kettle.

'Because, Mam,' I said, my voice and finger shaking as I pointed at the demon, 'the deal were only supposed to last a hundred year. It ended ten year ago.'

Mam and Da were struck speechless for a moment.

'But the Rector...' Mam started up.

'Likes us to be obedient.' I'd read it in his own hand.

'No, it can't be. H-he's such a kind man. Why would he...?' She slumped back in her chair, her eyes showing the churn in her mind.

'But if it is true,' Da said in an unsteady voice, 'if it's true, we put our bairns through this for nothing.' He were white with the shock, and I could see rage building in him.

The demon spread its hands wide. 'You can't blame us. Stuuuupid people with short memories make for gooood catttttle.'

'The feast is over, demon,' I said, hoping it would believe me.

'I'm not leeeaving,' the demon replied. 'In faaact, you have annnnnoyyed meeee. I might take you now.' It rose. Then it flickered, came at me fly-fast.

I lurched to the left, getting my feet half-tangled in the chair. I fell onto Da's shoulder.

'Annie,' he said, 'get away!' His strong hands pushed me behind him as he stood to shield me. From the corner of my eye, I saw a shadow arm swipe. Da flew. He hit the wall and slumped to the ground, boneless.

The demon grabbed for me. I backpedalled furiously, but it were like my feet were stuck in a mire. And the thing were fast, too fast. It grabbed my shoulders; searing pain as its claws sunk into the skin. Its hideous round mouth opened wide. Wide as a smile, wide as a yawn, wide as my face, wide as my head. It were going to eat me.

It lunged, then stopped, looked down. I followed its gaze and saw two shining, metallic points sticking through its chest. 'Iiiironnn!' It burst into a cloud of shadows and these fled under the front door. And there were my mother, standing there, my cartwheel-fixing mother, holding the meat fork from the roast in her hand.

She dropped it, gasping.

There were a terrible howling outside. Mam ran to the press in the corner and heaved out the bucket of nails to pour them on the threshold and windowsills. 'That should keep them out for now. If it doesn't, I'll stab 'em again.' She turned to me, and the look of horror reappeared.

'Your da!' she cried, and we rushed over to him. 'Lay him down flat,' Mam commanded and fetched some folded towels to put behind his head. Her hand looked burnt, like she'd put it straight in a fire, but all her attention were on Da. He looked bad.

He moaned and started garbling nonsense.

'Shush, dear,' Mam said softly. 'We're all right. You're all right.'

I looked behind me and jumped, but it were just the flickering of the candlelight. The demons were still moaning outside, but the nails were holding them off, so far. I started crying. Couldn't help it.

Mam grabbed me tight as we knelt there beside Da. 'Why didn't you tell us before?'

'Would you have believed me? Would anyone? Had to be this way, Mam. I'm sorry.'

'You're brave but you're a bloody stupid girl,' she said as she squeezed me. 'Don't ever do anything like that again!' And soon she were crying too.

'I won't,' I said. 'I won't have to. No one will. There won't be any more feasts once we tell everybody.' I confessed my secret research and everything the Rector's journals revealed.

The church had not made any more deals with the demons, but then, they hadn't needed to. People kept inviting them in, sure it were the right thing to do, and the priests just kept their mouths shut, pleased to keep the villages in fear, in line. What were a few kids dragged to hell compared to this?

'The little shits!' Mam said, and I were shocked. She punished swearing as hard as she punished stealing or lying. 'All the bairns going through that...' She shook her head.

'And you. And Da,' I said softly. 'All the parents round here.'

After a couple of hours, our eyes sore from watching for wisps of shadow coming in, the wailing outside diminished. Da slept.

'Reckon the dawn will see them off,' Mam said, 'It'll be here soon, pet. We'll see your Da right.' Then she looked at me. 'And then we'll tell everyone.'

She never says she's proud of me; don't need to. I know it. And I know what's going to happen. My Mam's a strong woman, it's true. But there are a lot of women like Mam round here. Said they were descended from the battle-queens of old. God help that rector, his bishop, and all the priests of the Uplands. God help any demons who try to snatch a kid again. They have no idea what's coming their way, now that the feasts are done.

THE SUN LINE

I **await the** Solar at the Ayr station with all the other travellers. The sea sends a strong breeze from the beach to keep us from overheating, and ribbons on jaunty boaters stream a sad farewell to holidays, and promenades, and fruit ices on the sand. I wear a sleek walking skirt with a small bustle, leg-of-mutton sleeves on my tailored jacket, and I clutch a travel guide. I also wear this face, this inquisitive, girlish face, and a modest hat secured with a hat pin that could vaporise the entire station within a nanosecond, should I use it in desperation. I pat it to make sure it is secure.

Unlike other trains, the Solar cannot stop, so we must be slotted in as our carriages pass. I wait on the smooth rotating pad. It will deliver me onto the running board like a waiter at the Grand Central with a drink on a tray. Officers of the Sun Line will run along the platform edge in front of us, leaping on, their forward motion seamlessly synchronising. Today they mustn't hang about. It is a sunny afternoon in late May, in this Diamond Jubilee year of Her Majesty Queen Victoria, and the train will move with dispatch.

I incline my head to the passenger who waits beside me, a matron from a well-to-do family. She returns the gesture slightly, gracing acknowledgement upon an ingenue. I am pleased she responds to the impression I wish to give – a girlish gadabout drifting back to the black smoke of Glasgow. I researched it diligently for this assignment.

I look past the matron to spy Lambda, waiting restlessly, further down the Solar's platform. Candy stripes, a dandy dapper jacket-and-tie combo suitable for a ladykiller. I frown. Surely a little flashy, a little anachronistic?

The tracks sing out to signal the train's approach on its return cycle from south to north, east to west. And then we see it: sleek brass and maroon housing in the front cabin peppered with bug strikes, a yellow dorsal stripe perforated by the doors that let out onto the running board, solar ray concentrators lining the roof. Glaswegian wags of the future will call it the Clockwork Lemon. But I prefer to call it the Solar – its name at birth, the Brockham appellation.

Lord Brockham was a visionary of his time. He saw the belching smoke of the coal-powered steam trains and decided it unacceptable to pollute the earth over which man had been given dominion. So, he invented the world's first transport powered only by the rays of the sun. And it was his gift, in perpetuity, to the people of Scotland. A train that never stopped. He created the cyclical track that loops from Ayrshire up through Glasgow to Edinburgh and back. And he requested it remain free for all passengers. It will not always be so, but today, in this time, it is.

The train nears, and the line of pads undulates passengers on board, like coins into a slot machine. I dart my eyes to the side as we move, only to see Lambda looking directly back at me. I look away quickly as if nothing has happened and cross the running board to enter. My opponent is in the next carriage, the one reserved for bachelors. Mine is the rear carriage for women and children. I choose to bide my time in the open seating as the Solar pulls away.

I am across from the matron, by chance. She reaches into her carpetbag and pulls out some embroidery, remarking, 'Such a lovely day.' I hum a note of agreement, hoping she will notice my posture, my gaze steadfastly locked to the view from the window and leave it at that. But, 'A young lady like you, unoccupied?' follows in a leading tone. "Unoccupied" can mean many things. I am not engaged in my own domestic pursuit – embroidery, or the like – or perhaps she means I should not have come from the seaside on a beautiful day. I should be caring for a brood of brats in a tenement, or a governess in a grand hall.

I face her, briefly. 'I assure you, ma'am, I am quite busy.'

She looks me up and down, her doubt clear on her face. I have no signs of make-work or motherhood apparent. The only thing I hold is a booklet, a well-thumbed, dog-eared prop.

'You are a reader, perhaps?' Her knitting needles are poised, waiting, and I see this question for the trap it is. She would subsequently assess my choice of material as scandalous, wastrel, or flibbertigibbet if it were a novel, gazette, or romance.

'Only of the Lady Traveller,' I reply, disappointing her with a flash of its cover. I cannot help myself. 'I find the chapter on avoiding irritating train passengers most enlightening.'

While she splutters for a rejoinder, I rise and breeze up the aisle, past children dressed in short trousers, or pinafores and pigtails, squeaking patent shoes; their governesses in severities of serge; the occasional mother, sadly watching a jolly day at the coast slip away while their babes-in-arms squall and puke. I cause a small disturbance behind me as I reach for the brass twist handle of the carriage door, exposing the rattling, noisy accordion guts of the train and the next door which opens into the forbidden lands of men.

In the interstitial space between carriages, I fix my appearance, and *change*, and open the door.

*

The century has turned. This carriage of the Solar is now hoaching with coal workers, manual labourers, mechanics. I wipe a black-nailed, rugged hand down the front of my work shirt and fish a tin of tobacco from my trouser pocket as an excuse to survey the passengers. I roll a tiny cigarette and light it. Some faces – moustached, grizzled – hide beneath caps brought forward. Some stare blankly at me, just another workman entering the carriage.

The Solar passes through Glasgow on this arc of its circuit. On any train, in any era, men perform for each other with over-loud banter and laughter. This one is no different. There is a storyteller, a working man's bard, regaling them with a humorous tale. He sits with his back to me. I feel sure it's Lambda, under the shaggy salt-and-pepper tufts of hair that peek out from beneath a dishevelled flatcap, dapper striped suit of yesteryear gone. I sit a few seats back and try not to look like I'm listening, pull out a new prop – a pamphlet on workers' rights – and pretend to read.

Lambda is telling them a slapstick story about a council meeting to plan the building of Cumbernauld. How this information got to the bard's ears is never quite clear, but the story holds some messages I can just make out underneath the humour. How Cumbernauld would become a dumping ground for Glasgow's slum dwellers. How it would rip the heart out of the city. I conceal my irritation poorly and choke a little on my dog-end of a rollup. A man next to me speaks.

'Can I borrow a fag?' he asks. I raise my eyebrow to look left. There is something about this man, his widow's peak, his eyes a little wild.

'Sure pal, but don't worry, I won't take it back when yer done,' I say drily and pass my tobacco tin.

He eases out a paper and teases out the strands of Virginian gold into its crease. He lights up with his own match, passes back the kit, and blows out his contribution to the blue fug in the carriage. He sighs and offers his hand in gratitude. 'Peter Manuel,' he says. The name seems familiar.

I clasp his hand while I access records, trawl through history from the time, and blanch with horror. He is a mass murderer who will be nicknamed the Beast of Birkenshaw, and in a few years, he'll hang in Barlinnie jail, one of the last capital punishments for a century. My mind scuttles while I recover my poise. He will hardly have noticed the pause, the small flinch in my hand as I remove it from his grip and place it over the penknife in my pocket.

'Tony Blair,' I supply, knowing this legend is safe from recognition for another four decades or so. But his very presence makes me feel uncomfortable in my skin, a prickling awareness crawling up my spine.

'You ever been inside?' Peter Manuel asks. I baulk at the question, despite my training and years of experience. He's wrong-footed me.

'Not had the pleasure of Her Majesty,' I reply, as smoothly as I can. In my peripheral vision, I notice Lambda getting up from his seat. I engross myself in the conversation, though it is a nasty piece of business. 'Why'd you ask?'

'Always nice to know someone clean,' he says and grins. The smile is death and decay. 'Could use a strapping bloke. Where do you stay?'

Lambda's exit to the next carriage is a welcome cue for me to get up. 'Sorry, got to go see a man about a dog.' But Peter Manuel does not drop his attention. I feel pinned in place by this man who annihilated entire families as they slept in their beds. The handle of the penknife in my pocket is cutting into my palm.

Finally, he smiles again, this time as if I'm made of glass, and he can see right through me. 'Take care, Tony Blair,' he chants, pleased with the rhyme. He winks, and I stutter a nonsense that might have added up to goodbye.

Sliding into the gangway and slamming the door shut felt like shedding my skin. I'll avoid that carriage the next time. While I'm here, I do shed my skin, anyway. And time. And gender. As always, the Solar goes round.

I'm beginning to hate this assignment. Every day the same. Follow Lambda. Observe. Report. I scope ahead, to find them, follow them, slip into the new timeline wherever they are.

*

Between Falkirk High and Polmont I am a young adult. This carriage is for scholars and clerks of state; this year's fashion is for ponytails for all genders wrenched up achingly high. The train slips past remnants of housing estates, and then we are back to the countryside. Agriculture now is not the agriculture of the past. No more monoculture, no more pesticides. An untrained eye might think it just an open woodland if it weren't for the slightly too-regular spacings between larger trees and smaller shrubs.

Lambda is spreading dissent again. 'Well, I heard that the Clockwork Lemon was invented in the 1950s and we were just told it was the Victorians to keep us from questioning the reasons the government shut down fossil fuels.'

The latest conspiracy. It doesn't matter that there are a hundred data point collectors out there in the ether that will follow this train through time, a million tintypes and photographs faithfully archived, flickering film of its inauguration – rumours from the throat of a "friend" are always more convincing. I must not intervene. Observation only. Though I dearly wish to run over and shake the nearest fresh-faced student and ask them to think for themselves, it won't do to break my cover.

I satisfy myself with getting my air-stylus out and stabbing it into the holographic icons in front of me. I could easily turn the object on Lambda, if I need to. Hatpin, pen knife, stylus, all the same function. A weapon from my time, disguised.

I see that one of the wide-eyed crowd is Mercy McDonald, once and future leader of the Scottish Free State party. If Peter Manuel imprinted evil on the multiverse, I can only hope that Mercy McDonald imprinted too. She asks Lambda some probing questions.

'But if that's true, how come more folk don't know it?'

'Listen, anti-fossil fuel lobbyists have got deep pockets. Vested interests.'

'But so many scientists agree that the long-term effects of petrochemicals on our world would have been devastating...'

'Well, a scientist I trust is saying something different. Listen, coal and petrol are much more efficient. We'd be able to go faster. Get from Glasgow to Edinburgh in a third of the time. Get it? Anyway, yous should just do your own research.' He tosses the virtual ball of electric blue into the air, and the scholars latch onto it. Poison spread, Lambda moves on. As I move to follow my target, I look back on Mercy, eyes lighting up from the inside with that same blue glow. What damage has been done? I move to the next carriage and find the answer.

*

Between Linlithgow and Edinburgh, I join a carriage of special polis, the 'Spesh'. Units of police with extraordinary powers were deemed necessary after the People's Corporation of Glasgow divorced itself from Holyrood's apron strings. There is a unit of Glasgow Spesh here, guarding a dignitary cloistered in an opaque privacy cubicle. The Spesh are louche, supercilious. I dress as one of their own, ranked at just above a constable, but far below where someone might have actually heard of me. I carry a gun openly on my hip. (It is not a gun, but it is.)

Lambda is there, as a lieutenant with a shoulder pip and contraband whisky in her hand. A sliding skin of amber-gold liquid coats the inside of the metallic tumbler as she swirls her wrist, practiced, casual. In between bawdy jokes with her comrades in black, she glances out the window at the barricades. Tires, barbed wire, oily gouts of flame from the petrochemical present haunt the view. Is she taunting me? I check this timeline's recent history.

The Solar is the lone vehicle allowed to pierce the line of black and orange fire that divides east from west in the central belt, the only transport between the Glasgow and Edinburgh city-states at this point in history. For the first time in millennia, we have allowed people we used to include in our image of *us* to drift fully into *them*. Our Sparta to their Athens, their Encyclopaedic

State to our People's Corporation. Oh, we've always had a rivalry; that's no surprise. Siblings often do. But like siblings, there was always a deeper loyalty beneath.

Until this timeline. Facts and culture slide into my head, harvested from the now.

Only the Spesh and diplomats may pass through this divide between the two. My target flicks me a comradely salute, and I almost sneer. But I must return the salute to maintain cover, and I do so with icy formality.

'Here, Officer,' she calls. 'Drinks are on me.' She pulls out her hip flask and another metal tumbler. I'm caught in her offer. The other Spesh look at me expectantly. They think the gesture is friendly, one Glaswegian to another.

'Spirit alcohol is illegal,' I say and cite the regs by reading them off a handheld device, quoting subsection and paragraph.

'It ought to be illegal no' to have a bit of fun sometimes,' she says, and I grit my teeth at her fake accent. Can't the others hear it? I sit down some seats apart instead, eyes locked forward. I check who is inside the diplomatic box. It is Ang Ross, on their way to broker a deal with the Cyclos for an agreement. The founder of the Pan-Scotia Space Agency. Contemporaries have fun with the acronym "PSSA".

Lambda keeps trying to engage, provoke. Or am I reading too much into her manner? She puts her boots up onto the seat next to me and drawls, 'I wis jist saying to these wans about the space elevator, 'n how it'll collapse on Prestwick toon.'

Protocols flash behind my eyes. This is an intervention point. Interference in the development of the space elevator, and the leg-up it gives us to the stars, is a red line.

'Sounds like Cyclo talk,' I say, and leave the notion hanging in the air.

The Encyclopaedic State took Dundee, post-split. The People's Corporation annexed Aberdeen for the teaspoon of offshore oil it had left. They took the embattled north of England; we bundled the Irish states to our bosom, best pals. Little territory grabs and scuffles seemed important for many decades. But now a deeper calling had us looking up. And it cannot fail. Prestwick once had claim to fame for the only place in Scotland where a singer named Elvis ever set foot. Now it claims the stars. And the Cyclos can't be having with that. It's gone beyond the pale. It's East versus West as always, ever anon, and on and on.

'Only a joke,' Lambda says with a sneer. 'Where's yer sense of humour?'

'My mum lives in Prestwick,' pipes up another Spesh, and Lambda's spell is broken. But this game has gone too far now.

She rises. 'I needed a pish anyway,' she says, and heads to the carriage door, past Ang Ross' cubicle. I follow, ruefully.

Another change, another carriage. I need to make a call. My supervisors on the Board of Intelligence ingest my report, send their blessing for my engagement request.

*

Spring-green leaves that look like grass blades swish by the next carriage's windows. For a moment is as if the train is floating, flying sideways above sugar cane fields. But then the eye rights itself. We are into the bamboo groves, the age of carbon sequestering. The fast-spreading species constantly threatens the track with its lightning growth. The door I lean on as I smig it closed is also made of bamboo, my clothing spun from its softened fibres, and its shoots have superseded the potato in basic carbohydrate consumption. The only other carbon capture plant more abundant is seaweed, a function of the vastness of the ocean. On land, this slender, overgrown reed has formed a scaffold for our society.

We're on the back swing from Edinburgh to Peebles and there's still some way to go.

'Of course, bamboo is really terrible for our native animals. What's left of 'em, anyway.' Lambda tells this to a woman wearing glowing green earrings. Her jewellery-fashion indicates she has permission to procreate, a rare gift in the scaled-down humanity of today. She is captivated by Lambda's new appearance – a masculine face of cut-glass cheekbones, broad shoulders, slender hips.

My approach causes a look of irritation to flicker over her face – she won't share attentions with anyone, but she relaxes as she notices I wear no procreator indicative jewellery, dress as non-binary.

A finely woven bamboo net holds my hair up into scrolls and curls, and the drape of my large-sleeved top and wide-leg trousers hides my weapon efficiently. In this reality it is an ert gun. I can fire a sliver of phasic material through Lambda's neck and it would degrade instantly leaving no trace. Perhaps I could be justified in reporting to headquarters on his demise. Of course, the woman might still see my arm rise then fall, and note the co-incidence of her conversational partner dying at the exact same time. She'd mark me as an assassin, and then I'd have to kill her too, and that would be... temporally complicated. I could look up who she is, who she will be or who she may parent, why Lambda is messing with her, but I no longer care. Time's up.

The carriage is almost empty apart from us. Sitting so close is a direct contravention of the Board of Intelligence's standing orders, but I have followed

Lambda for centuries, through genders and class. I'm sure they know who I am. It's time to make a move.

'Do you know what you're doing?' I ask aloud, and the woman mistakes it for a conversation with her, and before she can ask me what I mean, I hold up a hand, eyes locked with my opponent. We stay like this for a moment. I dart my eyes to the next train car, will Lambda to follow me as I make for the door, to a time of my choosing? I know they can do it, just as I could follow them.

Quick change, all change.

*

Pop music blares as I enter the carriage, my hair spiked into a crown. Disaffected youths display their boombox, sitting proud in its own seat on a packed commuter train filled with tutting businessmen, prim pensioners, and late-home private schoolkids who sway to the beat. The lowering sun has made the Solar sluggish, but it has a caboose-full of batteries to keep it going. I push up the sleeves of my denim jacket and place fingerless-gloved hands on the waistband of my rara skirt, feeling for my butterfly knife tucked in there while I tap one Doc Marten impatiently.

By the time the carriage door creaks open, the pop has turned to anarcho-punk-ska and some of the teens are attempting to pogo to the slow sway of the train, falling into each other and drawing the ire of the middle-class adults, laughter from the kids.

In this stretch from Douglas to Auchinleck, we are in the times where excess, consumerism, and nihilistic capitalism reign. But the Solar goes on, even when its interiors swelter under spraypaint signatures, and the stink of cigarette smoke and sadness.

'I'm here,' Lambda says, and I notice with a lurch of surprise that they look like no-one I've ever seen before. They are preternaturally beautiful. And out of time and place. They raise a hand and click their fingers, casually, causally. The last carriage of the Solar ripples and transforms into a white, clean, empty space. No more pogoing teens, no bamboo, no Spesh or workmen, no gaggle of governesses. We have stepped out of time and place to an artificial reality. 'You may as well relax,' they say. 'Be yourself.'

All my training and years of experience scream at me, but I've a decision to make. I drop my façade. We are here, we are now, we are us. 'Lambda,' I say. It is an acknowledgement.

'X', they reply. I breathe a slow exhalation of relief. No more pretence that we didn't know each other, that we haven't been watching each other over the centuries. 'What did you want?' they ask.

'You need to stop,' I say, nearly tripping over my tongue. To speak so bluntly to the ear of the Eternal Empire of Edinburgh is one thing. To make myself the mouthpiece of the Universal Reality of Glasgow another. But it is necessary.

Lambda blinks lashless eyes, as if confused by my – our – request.

'Your interference in the timelines,' I clarify. 'You're building up too much tension, you're going to make us jump track.' I am aware it is a train metaphor. It's apt, though.

Lambda takes on a sly expression, snakes their head to the side. 'But what would you do?'

'You brought back fossil fuel consumption! Sent us spiralling towards global climate disaster!' I threw up a display of the little changes Lambda had made, and their iceberg-melting effects. 'Then you threatened the Prestwick Stellar Express! Unacceptable!'

'But I had to. It was my duty, one my leaders set me to do. As yours did to you.'

'But how could yours possibly justify this action? It's bizarre, inhuman!'

'They told me this: "Our conflict has sent humanity to the stars, to walk through time and space. Without Glasgow, Edinburgh would not be what it is. And the reverse is also true. We need to keep bumping together, rubbing each other the wrong way. The friction produces sparks. Imagine what we could do if the conflict is deeper?" That is what they told me.'

They're suggesting this cold time war is somehow healthy for us, our development. I shake my head and bite back frustration. I speak slowly, deliberately. 'We have ways that allow us to see the parallel routes through time. The ones you might make us switch to. We can show you this at least.' I sketch a window in the air, all the communication a sensible agent would permit, no mind-to-mind contact. Not yet, at least. 'Watch the histories we passed by instead of through. That we nearly fell into.'

They flick forward and back with a musing finger through the selection of timelines I have curated. They scroll all the way back to before Brockham, then forward again, into the periods without the Solar. The train is unique to this one vibrant pathway. The other timelines are so different. Lochs of black sludge, granite hillsides melted like slag, air thick with brown fug. Dead places. Derailed. Wrong. Dead.

They frown.

'If you're right, we'll have to develop the ability to check.' Chagrin. We have invented something even they have not yet fathomed. Walking through our own past and nudging things about is one thing, but other pasts? Not so easy.

'Please do,' I say, and I wonder if there is a hint of triumph in my voice. 'We think you'll agree. Let's keep the Solar, keep things the way they are.'

Lambda nods and sends us back.

*

We're just coming back to Ayr station, circle nearly complete. It's a different time again. Lambda is male, uniformed, a bushy moustache with waxed curled ends, a bunnet atop his head. I am similarly disguised, kilt and jacket, stockings and flashing – this carriage carries troops returned from the Great War back to their homes by the coast. The train slows, and the soldiers rise, stiffly, and pull down their packs from the luggage racks, their eyes tired as if they, too, had walked through centuries. They adjust their faces, for they will meet their loved ones, and the horrors of war must be put away.

We all shape-shift, sometimes.

Lambda and I step to the running board, together, this time. We are disgorged from the train into a swirling gust of west coast rain, fingers of cloud pulling down from the sky as if to clutch at us. I clamp my bunnet to my head.

When I'm on the outskirts of town, I'll skip across the years and miles and walk home to Glasgow, no more Solar for today. No more crossing time and space after this one last effort, I've a bidey-in waiting for me in a tenement in Battlefield, and a brand-new leather recliner, and a book to read. I don't feel guilty for my decision to make my home in that era of self-indulgence. Let me enjoy it while it lasts.

Time to get up the road.

Lambda lifts his hat and nods, once, and no more words need to be said. Then he drops his façade and withers the air into a wee portal back to Edinburgh. I walk towards the Station Road, towards home, hunched up in the cold. The Solar rails sing again, music that fades into the mist.

THE FIRST EVER TAPESTRY ON STATION 17

Warp

There was a diary to record, a companion to her piece. The Arts Council had advised it could be in any format – a holographic skein, flat vid, audio – but Mhari chose the written word. It was less efficient, less personable, but she couldn't imagine her cramped and tremulous voice or thoroughly middle-aged face and body would enhance anyone's experience. No, let them see her in their mind's eye through these words, and the work.

Let only those who read to the end understand completely.

Weft

It is an honour for my art to be selected; I know this. I know also it will be difficult for earthbound me to make this work. But I have a holoskein to help me calculate how my tapestry will behave in microgravity, and, besides, I have to think about you all up there, working hard to help us overcome the environmental disasters we have brought down on ourselves. So brave of you to leave your homes and struggle up into orbit.

This is the art piece on which I will stake all my inheritance, family old and new. Where I've come from and where I want to go. Let me explain.

Warp

The loom Mhari used took up most of the space in her living room. She'd grown so used to moving around it, but the act of creating a diary jolted it into her foreground. There was a sofa, but that was currently covered in her art supplies, and was half unusable in any case, thanks to the loom's overhang. It was one of the reasons she still lived alone, even though she had long-term partner. It just took up so much space.

Huh, space. The thing she was creating would go up into a different kind of space.

Weaving would be only the first stage of the life of the tapestry. Once this stage was finished, there would be felting, embroidery, more and more stitching and embellishment. But already, there was a line-by-line picture coming into view, scanning, like the first televisions. There was the spirit of her childhood dog, Eddy, among the reeds that would bend and dance in the microgravity. There, her mother, tall and stern, in the largest of the drowned trees. And there Rachel, behind everything; a soft dove grey like the clouds she saw through her skylight, the light of Scotland and of home.

Weft

I chose a landscape as the only thing I could possibly send into space. Some might say a decorative theme is worth less than the abstract mastery of the New Greats.

But the art traditions are built on so many homages, canons, and insider information, that only the truly trained may see more than the outline. Thus, I chose one of the earliest forms of communication – an image taken from our own existence.

You were all born on Earth, so far. You all have this in common with me.

Why an artist in physical media? The work is two-dimensional in an age of holoskein entertainments that you wrap around your senses; it is something you will need time to appreciate, not an instant gratification. My tapestry invites someone to imagine a whole range of perceptions; touch, warmth, texture, even the soft smell of cottons and wools. And the landscape itself is mournful, bringing unease into an artform that used to epitomise ease, hung on walls of the rich.

But finally, it is to touch on parts of Earth that you may miss, up there in space. Have I made it too sad? Perhaps, but there is beauty and love in sadness too. And before the mission went to space, you might have looked at this landscape with complacent eyes. Now all the wealth of the biosphere, even a swamp with dead trees, will look startling, different than you remember. This heart-provocation is what I hope to bring to you. I hope it works.

Warp

She snapped a thread. It was going to be ruined. A cacophony of voices tumbled up in her head, bringing back the time when she lived in fear, walked on eggshells, a time of abuse. One small mistake, a splash of tea on the table, a frown where a smile was required, the wrong word. She'd learned how to placate, how to obfuscate, how to deflect the towering tirade that accompanied failure. She'd learned that homes were not the kind of place a person found comfort. That the people who are supposed to be sanctuary can be misery. And that they can tell you what you are, if you'll believe them.

Kneejerk responses of self-recrimination and self-belittling used to self-soothe; when the only home you ever knew was a place of suffering, suffering became home.

But, thankfully, things changed. She picked up the thread and thought about a new family, one found. The warm arms of Rachael wrapped around her as she said, 'Don't say that about yourself. Nobody should have to feel that way.'

Rachael would say other little things all the time. 'You're wonderful. I believe in you. You can do it.'

Although she still didn't yet fully believe it herself, after years of practice divorcing her past, it allowed Mhari the space to carry on her task.

Weft

This tapestry is a message to those who don't know me. I wonder if you can guess who I am? Do I have kind eyes or hard? Do I laugh with abandon or hide behind a hand? Was I born to speak a version of English, or another of the myriad languages in the world? Do you know how many there are? Can you hold inside your head the infinite combination and re-combination of words and semiotics, machine codes, and in-group references that make up how we speak to each other now?

How much simpler, more primal, is this work? What does that tell you about us, you, me, the nature of the universe?

Warp

Mhari took a moment to stand back and look at the work, cup of tea steaming gently in hand. Now seemed the right time to move to the hand-embellishment phase. But perhaps first, she should eat. She would need to clear the kitchen table, wash plates and bowls, the detritus of a physical existence on the margins of a work that was so dense it absorbed life itself.

A message from Rachael chimed on her wristlet. A holographic smile, words which she heard in that indomitably cheerful voice, even as she read them, 'Still hard at it? Let me know when you come up for air.'

Weft

Why did I do this? A tapestry in a space station, surrounded by hard edges, clean surfaces. The work is fuzzy, a little unkempt in places, a proliferation of chaos. Organic, by nature and form. If you touched it, would the oils from your hands change it? Would you tear it by accident? Would this then be ruin, or contribution to the piece and its message? Will you have to be careful of it, ensure that none of the fibres float off into the ventilation? What would that mean to a station whose mission is to save the planet from itself? Can we save each other? Would we even try to step lightly around each other?

Don't worry, I'm assured this will not be an issue with your fine filtration systems, I just wanted you to think about it, to feel a little fear. Fear can be good, it can keep us alive.

Warp

Rachael came up with a bag of shopping; her boundless energy made Mhari feel like a ghost in comparison. She greeted her and unpacked a loaf of bread wrapped in paper. 'Are you nearly done yet?'

Mhari smoothed away a frown. 'Still elbows-deep, I'm afraid.'

'A difficult birth, eh?' Rachael laughed and Mhari wished she didn't resent it, wished she didn't flinch and automatically feel like a failure.

'You could say that.'

Rachael stopped unpacking and crossed her arms, picking up on the vibe, finally. 'I'd forgotten what you get like,' she said. Mhari felt a surge of defensiveness, but then Rachael came over and kissed her gently on the cheek.

'Call me when you're really ready,' she whispered and Mhari just nodded, fighting the urge to cry ugly tears. 'It'll be the best thing you ever made, you just wait and see.'

Weft

I also wanted to show there is more to classical fine art than old oil paintings and muscular sculpture. To show an artform that is soft, that comes from domestic tradition, is still capable of high skill, symbolism, and sophistication.

One hundred years ago, I could not have made these claims without persecution following for having the temerity to believe in myself or my gender. To value my own views. I would be called an uppity bitch, at the very least. At the worst, my mental health might have been driven to the point of breaking, or I might even have been killed, extreme as that sounds.

I am still cautious, even though those times are (supposedly) past. I must actively resist the temptation to temper my words, to diminish.

Every message you receive by experiencing this piece is intended. Intentional. The fabric may be yielding, but it can still strike you right to the core. If you take more than a moment to think about it, at least. Use every reaction as a spur to do better, be more.

Perhaps the piece will only take up a place in your mind labelled, "fuzzy, rectangular". That is not my doing, but yours. Shake yourself out, like a blanket. Do the work.

Warp

Finally, it was done. Was it? Yes, it was. She knotted the last thread and patted the tapestry a few times, an action as subconsciously ingrained as shaking the washing as she hung it out. She stitched the three large panels together along their sides to make an enormous single piece. It dangled off the kitchen table and puddled on the floor.

Dead trees, stark and drowned, a symbol of so much in this flooded world. But not everything was dead. A miniature ecosystem grew among their roots in the soft brown silt below the surface. Small fish, tortoises, and tadpoles hid and thrived in the water. A cormorant snaked its head out in the branches above, searching for prey, ready to dive and spear a silver-slipping fish. A highland cow wading, half in frame, half out, buffeted by the rain. A humorous character, showing that we must bear everything thrown at us with a quiet dignity, even while all around looks at us with derision.

Weft

The tapestry piece will not lie flat, hanging down a wall, as it does here. My holoskein shows me what it should look like in continuous freefall. It will be tethered, but still, it will come alive. The reeds will wave in the motion of each station crew's passing, friction in atmosphere, just like the wind. The branches will reach out, as if to ensnare. It will cover an entire wall, a blanketing ecosystem.

I wrap the tapestry in my arms and think about the journey it will go on, the jet of carbon emissions that will surge it up into space. There will be other things taken on that journey, but my work will contribute to the weight, the need to kill the world a little more. It is a funeral shroud, a gag, an executioner's blindfold. In some ways, it represents my own death.

We will always spend a little of the Earth, until we let go of our stubborn way of life, our destructive way of being human. We already took enough from nature to last us forever. Each thread of this, though made from recycled textile, still cost something. Each calorie of heat used to wash the used material clean, each gram of carbon to truck it across the country to me, each person that needed more food because they worked that little bit extra for this. The tapestry has added to the overall burden on the Earth's failing systems.

So, when you see this tapestry, imagine it stuffs itself down your throat, throttles around your neck. For it is your burden now, Station 17. You must never forget your work. Let us all breathe once more. Each time you pass this work in the corridor, and the reeds caress your skin, feel the hand of time. And give your all. Don't succumb to our human ability to let things go. If you do, this tapestry's threads will uncoil, and grasp you as you pass, until one day, ultimately, they will smother you.

Warp

'So how do you think they'll like it?' Rachael asked as she helped Mhari vacuum-pack the tapestry for dispatch.

'Oh,' Mhari said with a wry grin, 'they won't.'

Rachael didn't know how to take this, was preparing to argue that she was being too negative again, if the shadows on her face were anything to judge by.

'Don't worry,' Mhari said, before she could start, though she loved how valiant a woman she'd found in this life. 'They're not meant to. But some of them will *think*.'

As she stuck down the last flap on the transport bag, she allowed herself a grim smile at last.

Threading in

I am sorry if this unsettles you. It seems my entire life has been aimed at making you feel this way. Every choice, every mistake, every tear or cry of ecstasy I ever experienced lead me to here, to the place where I goad you with a tapestry piece. How ridiculous of me! How unreasonable! But it is true, and what I set out to do. For what is art, if it cannot make you uncomfortable? What is art if it cannot inspire you to save the world?
So, go save it. You've read enough.

AFTERWORD

Hiya. Let me explain.

Some folk might not be keen on this book because I wrote stories that featured female, or female-coded protagonists. Some might call it 'feminist' and brand me a man-hater (I do not, I promise). But to be honest, I just wanted to see women centre stage because I am one.

For the avoidance of doubt: trans women are women. Nonbinary people are valid. Any feminism that excludes trans women, sex workers, people of colour, people with disabilities, or any other intersectionality is not feminism. It is patriarchy in disguise.

The characters come from different classes, too. I hope people notice that as much as their gender. I featured other ways of life than my own, and I may have made errors. I hope I did not. If I have troubled anyone by making mistakes, I apologise.

Whatever your response, choosing women as protagonists in some stories should not be the end of the universe. If I made you feel anything, that is my job. I hope it was more positive than negative. If one story hurt you, I hope another healed.

And now, I have to ask a small favour.

We're ruled by algorithms these days. And marketing spend. We hear a lot these days about how people are paid, promoted, and treated in general in publishing. But what can a reader do to help authors? Some quite simple things, it turns out.

1) Review and rate. Even if you didn't like it.

There is a rumour that, to *certain giant publishing platforms,* any star rating under 4 equates to a negative review. So, if you thought this book was just okay but you don't want to torpedo my book because I am just one small author, please bear that in mind! Please add stars and written reviews wherever you buy the book, if you can. It's not a cheap or even profitable pursuit, even under the best of circumstances. And people buy from recommendations; it's just a fact of human nature.

2) Talk about it

You can use Goodreads, Twitter, Facebook, Instagram, and TikTok (among other outlets) to unload your opinions about this book. You can write blog posts, you can tell friends over coffee. You can make fanart, take a piccie on your phone of a few words for a fair-use quote you upload to your social accounts. It's all helpful. Make sure you link back to the book if you can! But if you can't, you can use the hashtag #UnderTheMoonEMF. Hopefully that will get people where they need to go.

3) Follow the author on social media

For me, you can go here: https://bit.ly/FollowEMF

Algorithms again. It's just a fact that authors with larger followings are pushed up higher than those who have a pitiful few hundred organically-grown real human fans.

You can follow all my social media on that one link. I use Twitter the most, followed by Insta. I'm a gobby, irreverent clown on one, and an art and nature-loving hippy on the other. Take your pick!

4) Go to signings, book festivals, conventions, and other 'meat space' events. You can support other authors *at the very same time*, as a cheeky bonus.

5) Buy me a coffee*. If you want. It's up to you. Go to the Ko-fi link https://ko-fi.com/bethkesh to add what is, in effect, a tip.

Thanks in advance for anything you decided to do. I mean, even that you read this far means something too.

E.M. Faulds

*Tip moneys may be used for things other than coffee, e.g. convention bills!

ACKNOWLEDGEMENTS

I could not have found the gumption to go forward with this project without the support and encouragement of many people.

First, as always: Doug, my other half and an absolute rock. I couldn't manage any of this nonsense without you. Thank you.

Cat Hellisen, an author the likes of whom I can only hope to grow up to be one day – for constantly reassuring me that actually, yes, I can write, and helping in every stage with huge amounts of work on their part. Cannot thank them enough!

Neil Williamson, TH Dray (more fantastic writers) for beta reading and such kindness; Peter Morrison, Jenni Coutts, Heather Valentine, Brian M. Milton, and the too-numerous-to-mention other fellow members of the Glasgow SF Writers' Circle for helping me improve. Many of these stories have been shredded and rebuilt stronger by a turn through the Circle. Hal Duncan for being my gateway drug to the Glasgow SF scene. This is directly your fault!

Anna Smith Spark for being an absolute star; Allen Stroud and Karen Fishwick, I heart you both so much for your generosity of spirit. And to all the lovely people at cons who welcomed this random woman in.

Shona Kinsella, my liege! May your reign be both peaceful and long.

Uh, all the rest of my family and friends, you know who you are and what you did. If you don't, just ask. I will tell you!

Cheers.

ABOUT THE AUTHOR

E.M. Faulds was born in the Australian Outback and grew up on a cattle station. She spent her childhood walking through that landscape, telling herself stories.

She came to Britain on an adventure when she was seventeen and never went home. She now lives in Scotland with her husband in the oldest house in town, not far from Glasgow.

She's a member of the Glasgow SF Writers' Circle and host of Speculative Spaces podcast. She's had short fiction published in Shoreline of Infinity and Strange Horizons magazines, and a novel, Ada King.

Find out more about her here:
https://bit.ly/FollowEMF

Follow the discussion on social media by searching the following hashtag: #UnderTheMoonEMF

Printed in Great Britain
by Amazon

39166991R00118